I0518310

Cleo

Hiag Akmakjian

riverrun

Copyright © 2016 Hiag Akmakjian

Published by riverrun publishing, LLC 2016

www.riverrunpublishing.com

All rights reserved

No part of this book may be reproduced in any form or by any electronic or mechanical means including information storage and retrieval systems, without permission in writing from the author. The only exception is by a reviewer, who may quote short excerpts in a review

ISBN- 978-0-9982491-0-0

for Margaret –
with love

"That I make poetry and give pleasure – if I make poetry and give pleasure – it's because of you."

Quintus Horatius Flaccus

5 March

The Deux Magots and the Café de Flore: these are now the two popular existentialist cafes in Paris. Everybody goes there and I even saw Simone de Beauvoir having tea there one afternoon and felt sorry for her sitting alone.

It has been quite cold recently but today began with a pleasantly brisk morning and Jay and I were sitting outside on the terrasse of the Magots, the only people out there at that hour. I'm pretty sure the early-morning patrons inside on their way to work were viewing us as two crazy Americans freezing out in the cold. It only takes one breeze for the French to think they're all going to die of the flu. It was a bit chilly but not as bad as recently when a cold wave hit crops across northern Europe and the Dutch, who had suffered greatly during the war, were forced to eat their tulip bulbs. Although the war with the Nazis is now two years behind us, corpses in Germany are still turning up in the ashes of bombed-out buildings and reburied in cemetery grounds so frozen that new graves are being dug with explosives.

We were discussing cultural differences and the usual bullshit about life, with Jay commenting that the significant moments of life pass without our noticing them. For Jay life, of course, means women, his favorite topic, not to say obsession, and he was telling me about a young art student recently arrived from the States.

"Very good looking. I was surprised when she asked if I had read Tolstoy and if so which book and what did I think of it. It was like taking a qualifying exam for puss-ihhh."

"And you flunked."

"I definitely flunked. I don't know what she was looking for but I certainly didn't have it. I think maybe it's that I'm from New Orleans and she's from up no'th."

With his drawl New Orleans comes out as N'Awlins.

(Where he's living now is a Parisian quarter called MOAN-p'naahsse.)

"I'll introduce you," he says. "You'd probably make out."

"I've never read War and Peace. Not all the way through."

"Hey, even Tolstoy never read it all the way through. In one of his diaries he says he'd bang the upstairs maid whenever he got stuck about what to write next and that gave him the courage to go on. A good boff cleared his brain. Toward the end he got so bogged down he had to ask the maid what she thought the ending should be. Most people don't know this about Tolstoy. War and Peace was originally called War and Boffing but the publisher made him change that. He said he could sell more copies if the title didn't include the word "boffing".

Jay: in full stride now.

Me: "A writer? – with an upstairs maid?"

"A writer and a Russian count," Jay said. "In those days Russian counts had upstairs maids for boffing purposes. Before TV and movies the only thing to do when you got snowed in for six months was ring for the maid."

"Poor woman."

"No, she liked it" . . . and on and on and on, full tilt, Jay at his best (recording these bits for later).

I asked him where the Tolstoy girl was from. I had been looking to meet somebody new after a recent fling with an artist's model, a farm girl up from the Auvergne. Nice girl, Beatrice. She was not looking for sex, she said, not by itself, but sex combined with love. Very French, that, the French always talking about love. But she had a superior manner and there was no way I could fall in love with her. I liked her uninhibitedness in bed but after a week knew things were not going to work out.

I teased her about love and how the French were always talking about l'amour, l'amour toujours.

I asked her "What is love?" and she said a little primly that I'd know it if I were ever lucky enough to find it. Almost walked out on me at that point. But the trouble was she liked sex too much and could never get enough of it, so much so that I was sure she was seeing someone else on the side – or maybe I was the someone else she was seeing on the side.

Jay, still on the Tolstoy girl, thought I should meet her.

"From Connecticut," he added.

I was curious. Curious because Jay almost invariably made out and here he was passing a new prospect on to me. (To Jay women are "prospects".)

"What happened?"

"The subject of sex came up."

And of course that made me laugh. "Just like that. The subject of sex came up."

"She said she was sorry but she doesn't put out."

"She said 'I'm sorry but I don't put out'."

Hearing me laugh now started him laughing too.

"She said that where she comes from people don't go hopping in and out of bed. I said I told her I couldn't imagine what part of planet Earth they might be living on. New England – can you believe that? I pointed out that even in New England there had to be a certain amount of hopping in and out of bed, seeing as how the population was increasing and it wasn't all just Europeans getting off the boat. She said I sounded very immature."

"So what happened?"

"Nothing happened."

"Nothing happened?"

"It sounds freakish but she wasn't interested in me. I said to her, 'What do you want out of life?' She said, 'What do I want out of life? I'm not sure what I want out of life. What do you want out of life?' I told her I wasn't sure either."

3

"There's a knockout in my hotel," I told Jay. A beautiful girl, a real stunner. "She's something I'd want out of life."

"From Brittany," he said. "Tall blonde, right?"

I wasn't surprised he knew who I meant. Jay had briefly stayed at my hotel before I moved in – in fact was the one who told me about the Hotel du Dauphin.

So we batted the tall blonde around for a while, agreeing about a certain sensual quality she had. The first time I ever saw her was when we were passing on the stairs, she with two lean six-foot-tall Africans with high cheek bones and the whitest teeth I had ever seen and skin so black their faces glistened like wet coal. The almost corkscrew stairwell of the Dauphin is narrow and the four of us twisted sideways to get past each other. As I continued down the stairs and looked back I saw her wiggling her ass at the man below, who obviously enjoyed the cancan show, as she grinned promisingly at the man above. I imagined the fun they were about to have.

"Hard to get close to, though," Jay commented. Seeing me now thinking about her he said, "You writing all this down?"

"I'm an art student," I said. "A painter."

"Art student – painter. Yeah sure." He laughed.

We were both enrolled at the same art academy. He knew I was there only to enroll at an approved school in order to qualify for the GI Bill and its monthly subsistence allowance. It's what made it possible for me to live in Paris.

He was looking at me with an intense gaze.

"What do you write about?"

"Things."

"Just things?"

"Different things."

"Any of it published?"

"Not yet."

"Well," Jay said, shoving his chair back as he got up. He had to go see somebody on the Right Bank.

"Good luck," he said. He'd see me later at the Pommier. That's the art school we're both attending. The Académie du Grand Pommier, named, I believe, for an old apple tree that had once stood there.

After Jay left, the waiter came out to ask if there was anything else. I wasn't ready yet to start the day so I ordered another cappuccino just to sit there a while. A big clunky green-and-white bus, an ancient juggernaut that must have dated from the 1920s and still in service because of the war, came roaring down the rue de Rennes toward the Deux Magots honking its Bombay klaxon as it crossed the square. On the open rear platform I could see a woman with her arm up and hanging on, swaying with the bus as she yanked the chain ka-CHING to be let off at the Église St. Germain. The bus lurched to a halt, comically pitching the woman forward and violently back again. She hesitated a moment before stepping off the bus, moving with care.

Points to Remember:

The couple at the corner saying goodbye at the top of the Metro steps, he with his hands in his overcoat pockets as she gives him a peck on the lips before skipping down the steps and smiling back at him. Tableau: a happy night together.

Two schoolboys meeting briefly, shaking hands and going separate ways. French politeness begins early. Everything's done with a handshake. You enter a room and shake hands, you leave the room and shake hands – handshake-handshake. At my hotel the owner's wife and I meeting once on the narrow stairs, she squeezing past, arms loaded with parcels and with a musical laugh extending her elbow to me. Primly gripping the elbow between thumb and forefinger I tugged her arm down and up once, a metaphorical handshake, and, courtesy mutually preserved, she continued on her way.

The poster near the Métro entrance advertising girdles. The

text said something about the girdle causing a scandal or maybe the girdle was called Scandale. The topless model wore the advertised girdle, her pastel-colored breasts an artistic haze. In New York she wouldn't be shown with bare breasts, even paled.

The waiter came back out with the cappuccino and asked in English:

"You are from London, yes?"

"No, New York."

"Ah!"

To confirm an impression, he asked if I was a veteran of the recent war. Yes? Ah, he had been sure of it!

"Les nazis, hein? La sale guerre."

A head shake for the two of us – that filthy war. He said he had observed me studying the spire of the Église St. Germain and explained – speaking French now, enunciating slowly to a foreign visitor – that the church was très ancienne and a fine architectural example of something or other, I didn't quite catch what, and asked if I understood what he was saying. I nodded to be polite.

"Très ancienne," I said – communication effected.

"Yes, the oldest church still standing in Paris. Did you know that?"

I did not.

It was a fact few people knew.

It had been built a thousand years before the discovery of America. His eyebrows shot up at this revelation – hein?

In guidebook English and with many voilàs and a few heins thrown in he explained that in the year 542 – writing the number on the back of his check pad to show me ("Hein? 542? voilà") – Paris was two islands in the Seine. The Left Bank, where we were now, had once been a grassy meadow. Le pré aux clercs. Gently sloping down to the river? hein? Voilà.

He translated pré into English: "May-dough."

I was happy to be understanding key words like philosophe, as when he spoke of René Descartes – le philosophe? – voilà. He was buried in this church. Did I know that the philosopher René Descartes was the man who invented roulette? If today we go to Monte Carlo and play roulette, it's thanks to the philosopher Descartes. He looked at me expecting a reply.

"Ah," I replied bilingually.

From my pocket I placed a loose collection of French bills on the table. The thousand-franc banknotes looked like the work of the first-prize winner of a School of Fine Arts annual competition. The smaller-denominations were old currency printed before the war. They were worn to limp faded rags barely kept in one piece by gummed paper.

Not being sure how much to leave as tip for the history lesson, I motioned for the waiter and fellow combatant to make a selection from the bills I spread out on the table. With care he pushed the thousand-franc notes over to one side looking at me meaningfully as he did so. Those – no. Having thus established personal integrity and financial disinterest he continued, pinkie curled, delicately fingering through the rest and holding up for my authorization a couple of the smaller tattered bills that looked like they'd been through the laundry a few times.

I nodded general assent and he said "Merci, m'sieur!" with such fervor that I felt a surge of happiness for him. Now with feelings of wartime camaraderie even more solidified by this show of monetary appreciation of services rendered, he wiped the table with an operatic swipe of his serviette followed by a smart snap! – and again said, "Merci, m'sieur!" – and I wondered if I might recklessly have overtipped him.

Later

As I pass Mme Verger's loge she sings a musical hello. She seems very friendly.

She has a bizarre notion of New Yorkers. New York has exotic appeal for her. With commercial cheerfulness she tells me how well-mannered and courteous New Yorkers are, ah les new-yorkais!

"And you're a veteran of the recent war! Ah that filthy war, hein?"

I come away with two impressions. First, to speak fluent French it is obligatory to throw in several heins? per minute along with a sprinkling of voilàs. Second, Mme Verger doesn't have the slightest idea of what New Yorkers are like.

I remember that I forgot to ask Jay where he knew this Tolstoy girl from and how we could meet or somehow bump into each other. He had mentioned a milk bar, Chez Patrick's – or was it the Dôme she went to? Patrick's Milk Bar is a cutesy café directly across the boulevard from the Coupole where I sometimes go for the best-tasting espresso around.

Afternoon

As I'm writing, Justin, the valet de chambre, comes back for a change of towels. He forgot this morning. His day normally begins at the top of the hotel, the seventh floor, the sixth by European count, and my room gets done first. The top floor was once apparently an attic and has just two tenants, myself and a middle-age Romanian professor at the Sorbonne. He wears thick glasses, has a pleasant voice and smiles a lot.

My room has the feeling of a former maid's room – chambre de bonne. Actually it's just a top-floor attic room fancied up for renting. What gives it a cozy feeling are the flouncy white curtains framing a dormer window.

Justin is always glad to see me, probably because having someone to talk to makes his routine less boring. With the bed made he scrubs the sink and checks the bidet and I try not to get in his way but use the opportunity to practice speaking French. In exchange I learn about the Latin Quarter and French history. He's very talkative and loves teaching French history. Had I noticed the recessed top stories of buildings that tilt in away from the street? That was Baron Haussmann's design. Baron Haussmann? He was quite a figure, the prefect of police under Napoleon III and the one responsible for the big makeover of Paris. The Paris we know now? It's all his work. Those narrow streets that run into boulevards at sharp angles like cake slices? Do I know why? It was so armed troops could flush insurgents out into the wide boulevards where the waiting cavalry could annihilate them. They were picturesque in their angularity, those streets, hein?, but there was that tactical scheme behind it.

6 March

I like my hotel. Before I found out about the Dauphin from Jay and moved in I had looked at other hotels in the area, including one where the concierge swore that her hotel was absolument bug-free and I could ask anybody I liked if I didn't believe her. So I skipped that one, and skipped another that had wallpaper that all but came off the wall and shook hands with you: thousands of huge cabbage roses intertwined with pink rococo leaves and apple-green scrollwork ending in little tendrils and curlicues of mustard rose – a nightmare. One sunless room, briefly inspected, had walls twice as tall as the room was wide, a good room for one last look in the armoire mirror before putting the pistol to your temple.

I knew I would rent where I am now when I looked out the window at the chimneypots and slate-blue roofs that seemed only meters away and almost touchable but were the opposite side of the narrow street. It was Stock Photo No. 1: "Rooftops of Paris" – a lone geranium in a flowerpot and a black-and-white cat on the roof's one small patch of sunlight. As I looked, the cat gazed back squint-eyed, our two consciousnesses meeting above a canyon of street, the Rue Bonaparte.

Mme Verger's lively eyes tracking my inspection followed my looking at the cat.

"We are going to get a cat too."

"Do you have mice here?"

"No no no no."

She concluded the tour with what sounded like her clincher: "Tous les conforts! et eau chaude – the water always hot even here on the top floor – toujours, toujours."

NOTE. Mme Verger and her husband, the propriétaires of the Hotel du Dauphin, are ardent royalists, a completely unexpected thing. That may account for Madame's short brown Joan of Arc haircut. She has a figure quite appealing for her age – upper forties? fifty? – and knows it.

Monsieur Verger is never without a broad silk cravat and discreet gold pin. And when he dresses up it's in his one suit. Heavy tortoise-shell glasses give him the swanky look of a French romantic film star. He walks as someone who has just received an invitation from the Comtesse de Paris and her town car awaits him down on the street, sixteen cylinders quietly purring.

The Vergers seem to approve of me and go out of their way to accommodate the young American locataire. Patiently they explain things so that the young foreigner from New York speaking only baby French can understand what they're communicating, or at least get the critical words. Learning that I'm a veteran of the recent war ("Veteran? So young! In France a veteran is someone old and retired") they have apparently concluded that I was among those who liberated Paris from les boches and earned the privilege of accompanying General De Gaulle in his victory parade down the Champs Elysées on the historic day of August 1945.

"Ah those days!"

But they're royalists. The blonde of the two lovers explains things to me:

"To French royalists, whatever happened in the past was good. It was all good. It was part of the greatness of France – la gloire, the glory that was France" – all except for one small episode: the unforgivable blunder called the French Revolution.

7 March

One of the hotel's two cabinets de toilette is at the end of the short hall. Dangling by a string from the wall are small torn-up rectangles of newspaper. They're the toilet tissues. That's bad enough: printer's itch.

Harder to get accustomed to is the damp cold of the closetlike room. Early mornings your breath puffs up in the light of a low-wattage bulb dangling from the overhead dark of a skylight painted black during the war.

I share the top-floor cabinet with the shiny-domed Sorbonne professor. He teaches either philosophy or philology – I never got it straight. In a daily ritual, he makes a trip to the cabinet to do what he has to do and stays for as long as it takes him to do it. I once saw him enter the closetlike room with a one-volume Larousse under his arm, noisily latching the door behind him, obviously in for a lengthy siege. Soon even from as far down the hall as my room I could hear muffled East European groans.

You learn not to visit the cabinet just after he's been.

8 March

Justin changing the sheets on my bed shows an interest in art. He asks about the golden section as used by the old masters in the Louvre. He'd heard that there's such a thing as a golden section.

He comments on a landscape I have been working on – or attempting. His head tilted, eyes narrowed, he assumes the look of an art expert judging a work and makes a quick movement of his chin toward the painting.

"It begins to have character," he declares encouragingly. "I like it. I like all of it but the green seems – the green could be a little less raw, do you see what I mean?"

"Should be a bit warmer?" I pretend to go along with him.

"Just a slight bit. Nothing obvious."

He is in his thirties and has an anorexic look. His moustache, a black line as thin as a surgeon's incision, follows the contour of his upper lip. It must take patience to maintain the thinness of the line.

Mme Verger recently told me of the terrible thing that happened to Justin during the war. The poor man tripped the wire of an anti-personnel mine – "of the kind most horr-eee-ble!" She shudders and from her description I recognize the antipersonnel device the GIs called a Bouncing Betty. It lies buried and when you accidentally step on it you trigger a grenade that rockets up a few feet before exploding at crotch level. In Justin's case instead of killing him it resulted in a freak accident that blew both his balls off in a single surgical slice that miraculously left his penis intact.

I can't be sure, of course, that there's any connection but I have the feeling that Mme Verger takes advantage of Justin's war injury to harness what she imagines must be the pent-up energy of the poor castrato and puts him to changing sheets, doing laundry, dusting rooms, vacuuming carpets, washing windows, scrubbing toilets, waxing furniture, polishing brass and, during what she calls his down time, making the family silver gleam. The hotel is certainly spotless, all because of a German land mine.

Newspaper clipping: "Art crime is ranked as the third highest-grossing criminal enterprise behind drugs and arms, with figures suggesting that in France alone in 1947 art worth more than $500 million was stolen from galleries and drawing rooms."

Newspaper headline: "Death Leads to Feelings of Isolation"

10 March

The Pommier is quite a school. It's in an old brick building whose interior walls are permeated with a turpentine odor so ancient it has mellowed into a honeyed fragrance. It's on a short side street of no traffic and you could easily walk past it, as I first did, without noticing the faded "Pommier" sign over the front door.

This morning the school was just opening up as I got there and Madame Rose gave her usual greeting from her small table inside the front door.

"And how goes the young American?"

Sitting at a tiny table Mme Rose collects a fee from people sketching models in the large ground-floor atelier, the studio that's open to the public. Other students, those officially enrolled, may use the ground-floor atelier without paying but only they may use the other five studios on the building's two floors and also the sculpture studio in the back.

The French students refer to Mme Rose as a numéro, an eccentric. She is a woman in advanced middle-age whose face is a network of superfine wrinkles. Her gray hair is pulled back to a coiled bun behind her head, giving her a certain chic. Even indoors she wears a small black straw hat and rising from the side of the hat a papier-mâché rose quivers on a wire that wobbles with her head movements. I think it's meant to be elegant, not funny. Her rouged and powdered face makes her look like a Toulouse-Lautrec cabaret artiste in his La Goulue period.

I remember that soon after I got to know her she confided that she had once had an affair with "the great Modigliani" – giving me a wink and asking if I wanted to hear about it. I was genuinely curious. Well, it wasn't exactly an affair – one should not exaggerate. No, what she had with Modi was more of a fling, although maybe fling was perhaps too strong a word. It was more of a one-night stand, but, mon Dieu! what a night!

Telling me this her face glows.

The school's administrator, Mme Charpentier, runs the place from an office next to where Madame Rose sits. Mme Charpentier is an energetic woman with a newly-started double chin and she too always wears a hat, looking as if she were just on her way out and you had caught her as she was leaving.

Students on the GI Bill sign in each morning as required by the American Embassy. Mme Charpentier keeps a large register lying flat open on her desk and obeys the Embassy's rules even though she is of the opinion that an atmosphere of regulations is not the proper way to treat artists. They need to be allowed to stray a little, go out to the country and paint from nature, or meet each other in cafés and discuss problems of art the way, according to her, Corot and Cézanne used to do. It's her opinion that talent brings with it a wildness in temperament that deserves the utmost respect and protection.

Mme Charpentier is flexible about checking attendance. One GI student actually lives a thousand miles away, off the coast of Spain. A fellow GI passes himself off for him, faithfully signing his friend in each morning and then walking over to the Dôme to start his day of drinking. No one seems to care that the absent student has worked out a happy life for himself in Ibiza, a far-off enchanted isle. For his GI seventy-five dollars a month he has a house on a cliff above the sea and what are for him the three essentials of life: a goodly supply of beans and flour, a wine cellar of cheap Spanish rojo and an all-purpose local girl to cook the beans, share the wine and warm his bed. A GI visiting him reported that the house had no indoor facilities and you started the day by taking a sheet of newspaper out to the edge of the cliff for a leisurely morning dump while gazing at the blue immensity of Mediterranean before rolling up the warmish bundle and choofing it over the side, avoiding calamity by checking first for wind shear.

In Mme Charpentier's absence, her twenty-year-old daughter, who was rumored to have happily come out as a lesbian at fourteen, sometimes acts as informal surveillant général. Madame's more usual replacement is Lucien, a prematurely balding retired Sunday painter whose old-fashioned specs keep sliding down his nose and being pushed back up again.

Lucien sees that the school runs smoothly and has general

charge of hiring models. Black potbellied stoves, going back to when Giacometti studied there with Bourdelle, burn egg-shaped coals molded from coal dust called boulets. The stoves are very big and keep the ateliers comfortable in winter.

All three – daughter, Lucien and Mme Charpentier – are equally lax about regulations and in the first warm days of spring everybody's leniency towards discipline degenerates into so cheerful a delinquency that sometimes not just GI students but the staff doesn't bother to show up except to unlock the front door in the morning and then wander off for a coffee and brioche at the Dôme, letting the school run itself. As it does anyway.

Nobody from the Embassy ever comes over to check the record except an occasional young staff member who might wander in on "official" business and enjoy gawking at the nude models. There's trust between Embassy and school and now, in the late 1940s, still an easy atmosphere in which the Americans are past the merci à nos libérateurs period of Franco-American amitié but beginning to be disliked out of dollar envy or a beginning perception of the ugliness of American arrogance, leading to the "Yankee Go Home" slogans painted on buildings.

But the wartime hands-across-the-sea feeling still holds, and possibly for this reason there are occasions when, just before the noon break, the member of the staff who happens to be on front-office duty that day comes back from the Dôme or grocery shopping, scans the student list and conscientiously signs all the GIs in, whether seen or not. That satisfies the two principals involved: the Pommier continues to enjoy monthly payments of U.S. funds per number of students putting in a daily appearance and embassy officials enjoy a well-done feeling for an excellent record of student attendance.

The model, already on the platform, waits to hear the class

monitor yell his comic ritual "À poil!" – "To the pubic hair!" The model calmly folds the page of the book she was reading (Autant en Emporte le Vent, Margaret Mitchell), stands up and lets her kimono slide from shoulders to platform and, kicking it to one side, turns to face the class with a hand-on-hip pose while staring into space. The room falls silent with now only the scratchy sound of charcoal against paper and the swish and thump of brushes on tightly stretched canvas.

The maître comes around once a week and speaks of la noblesse de la matière, or plays for laughs: "That's some ass you put on the poor woman. Do you see her as an elephant?" Sometimes the critique is a generalization: "Make colors lively. Colors should sing!"

Artists and Models

In the school's four ateliers there's a new model each morning and each afternoon, almost always a woman, with much physical variety in the female body, from pale anorexic torsos to chunky-legged forms and adolescent bosoms, women with hanging breasts and areolas the size of beer pads. Of the dozen new models each week some are from Copenhagen or London working their way to the Riviera. None would qualify in a beauty contest but are fascinating as a study in oversized hips or an absence of buttocks and other features normally concealed by clothing. In art classes anomalies are a plus – a bump on a hip or a mild asymmetry of shoulders – variations with aesthetic interest. There was even one model who posed often at the Pommier who had what the Queen of Sheba's pubic hair was said to be like, a fur triangle as huge as a sporran that grew down the inside of her thighs and thinned out as it reached her knees. There's hardly ever anything of the classic ancient Greek sculpture among the models, although very occasionally a woman of a good figure and looks will show up. Most of the models are women you see every day. Some look like well-built Courbet farm women and some are Pissarro's peasant girls, but none ever a match for Phryne, Praxiteles's model for Venus. Phryne, charged with corrupting the youth of Athens, defended herself in court by letting her toga fall to the floor to allow members of the court to see her in the nude and judge for themselves if her beauty was immoral. The judges took one look and acquitted her.

Only one model at the Pommier had a beauty that came close to Phryne's, a Norwegian lesbian who at first sight had male students feeling an acute yearning for her. Surprisingly, she especially liked posing for sculptors, which was the hardest kind of posing to do. Posing for a sculptor meant that for a week at a time you held yourself upright and unbudging or lay still on a low-to-the-ground revolving stand that one of the students turned a quarter-way round from time to time to study an arm or a leg close up or from a different angle. If the pose was one of the model lying on her side with a leg drawn up at the knee, the raised knee was supported by a block of wood. It was boring work, very hard on aching muscles, but most models seem patient and never complained.

There is still much unemployment and an oversupply of local women willing to disrobe. Before the war there was a Monday morning outdoor models market at the end of the street at Vavin, catty-corner from the Café Dôme, and it never lacked for women looking for work. It was a desperate time then. It still is.

Some models live en ménage with a painter and to earn pocket money for costly hard-to-get items like nylon stockings, pose privately for other artists. Many prefer private work, some liking it because it makes it possible to mix work with pleasure, the model finding no good reason for a session not to end in bed. The cliché of artists and models hopping into the sack is apparently not a myth, and in such cases, of course, the posing is sometimes done pour l'amour.

A month ago I ran to catch a bus and my reading glasses fell out of my lapel pocket. I found an optician on the rue de Rennes, Dr Yitzhak Heimowitz – middle-age, friendly.

Humming, he tested my eyes and on my return visit inquired about my accent. Ah, New York. Veteran? – Europe? Yes, Europe – Belgium, Germany. He settled the frame on my face, hooking the wings behind the ears and asked how that felt. Fine. "Bon," he said, smiling at our progress. I asked him how much. He looked at me almost tenderly. "I'll send you a bill," he said. No bill yet.

20 March

I asked Jay if the girl he wants me to meet is a student at the Pommier. Unfortunately, she's not.

Jay: "And by the way, whatever happened to that Sandrine girl?"

That was the model I had been seeing. For pocket money and for buying expensive things like nylon stockings, Sandrine did a little private posing for artists and approached me after a morning session at the Pommier and asked if I lived nearby and would I like to paint her privately. Barely inside the door she slipped out of her skirt and blouse and said, "I've never had an American."

She refused payment. It was true we hadn't done much work, but apparently a principle was involved, and also professional ethics.

"What do you take me for?"

"I thought I should at least pay for your time." But I saw her point and apologized.

"When I mix business with pleasure I don't take money," she said. Then half in English, half in French: "Eet eez done pour l'amour."

1 April

Bought Pepys's Diary at a bookstall along the Seine. Having a French wife waiting for him at home didn't stop the old boy from chasing skirts all over London. He complained that his wigmaker's servant would not laisser him faire l'autre thing – the reader's imagination filling in what l'autre thing he had in mind – though he did what he pouvait to have got her à laisser him . . . the tortuous language incidentally reassuring me that my own French was already an improvement over his, however slightly. But then to be honest, his was meant as a private code to hide his postings from his wife – although she being French could read French and so that didn't make sense.

2 April

Stendhal: "I went to Paris with the settled intention of seducing women." I can't think of a better reason.

The wall of the American Embassy in Paris: "Benjamin Franklin: 'Every man has two countries, his own and France.'"

Franklin, gentleman scientist, American diplomat, bon vivant, long-time resident of Paris, happy solacer of widows, described in a letter his last-minute failure of nerve when "being in Paris where the Mode is to be sacredly follow'd I was once very near making Love to my Friend's Wife."

The recent epidemic of grippe across Europe has excited a

resurgence of chauvinism. The English call it the French pox and shove the blame across the Channel. The French resisting a simple tit for tat and blaming the English shove it further south and blame it on the Italians. It's now the Italian pox. Or as the weekly satiric newspaper Le Canard Enchainé headlines it, "La Grippe Italienne – or All Roads Lead to Rum." Naturally the Italians feel unfairly treated and defend national pride by shifting the blame sideways to Spain. It's the return of the Spanish flu. I forget what the Spanish are calling it. By now everybody in Europe has a cold.

Tuesday, 15 April

Jay telling me his troubles with the French language. One of the first words he ever learned was fermé, meaning closed, and he sees it everywhere now. Restaurants are fermé between meals. The Louvre is fermé on Mondays. Shops are fermé during lunch hour. Some shops are fermé on Sundays and Mondays. Some are also fermé on saints' days and death-in-family days. Then there are always spontaneous occasions like inventory days.

"And of course all the sudden national holidays."

I remind him: "Plus, don't forget, the entire month of August."

"Right, fair-may!" he said. "France sees itself as a world power except that it's closed on Mondays."

HEADLINES

One-Armed Man Applauds the Kindness of Strangers

Psychics Predict World Didn't End Yesterday

Mayor Unveils Erection to Cheering Crowd

Woman Missing Since She Got Lost

Homeless Man Under House Arrest

A mix-up in mailboxes. In mine an outsized travel postcard date-stamped Nairobi addressed to a Martine Lecoeur. A crayon heart in hot pink is drawn around the name Martine.

This provides an opportunity for a neighborly chat. I knock on the addressee's door to hand-deliver the card. "Ah, c'est vous." Hearing my beginner's French, she inquires if I'm from America and whether I fought in the war. "And hein? you have come back now, after that filthy war, hein?"

My reward for the card: she flashes the sunniest of smiles that in my head mixes with an exciting sound of high heels clacking down flights of stairs. How Byronic, I think, to shack up with someone a few floors down.

We compare notes on the Vergers. She assures me they're all "gaga" and feels sorry for Justin, the poor bastard (pauvre con). Because when a man – her voice darkens here into a spooky hush of compassion – when a man in his prime has to face life deprived of certain of his y'know, appendages, awful things start happening to his brain.

"Y'know?"

(Hein?)

I attempt a pass at Martine and ask her out for a drink. She takes it with a smile – but no thank you. I was gentille and all that but the unfortunate fact was – and here her look changes to one of sympathy – I suffer from a fault that no amount of living will ever change. I have the wrong color skin.

Justin though an employee of the Vergers is included in the evening ritual of dinner, for which he dresses up in cuff-linked white shirt and tailored jacket when the ugly-duckling valet de chambre becomes an ancien régime swan to join Monsieur and Madame at table. As I pass the always open door of their lodge at the dinner hour I can hear a background radio softly playing a Mozart piano concerto as they dine. Which is what they do: The Vergers are not the kind of people who eat dinner – they dine. I begin to feel a fondness for a hotel run by royalists who are so democratic as to invite their domestic help to share their evening meal with them. Or it might be that the meal is in lieu of pay – that plus a rent-free room? Or perhaps the valet de chambre is also an ardent royalist.

16 April

Since being redecorated in earlier years, the walls of the top floor are thinner than normal. I realize this when I hear groans coming from the room of my neighbor, the Sorbonne professor. He appears to have a gift for enticing female students to his lair. I recently heard a woman's voice orgasming in guttural sounds that made me think of a death rattle, or how I imagine a death rattle might sound (fortunately never having heard one). The voices of his women visitors vary from a low growl to high-pitched screaming, and one regular guest is a memorable wall-banger with an upper register that goes off the charts. In English slang you come when you have an orgasm and in French you go away. And in the home stretch, judging by her rhythmic slapping and pounding on our shared wall, she crosses one or more time zones. As I picture it, she leaves the professor's room a deeply fulfilled woman and, as I imagine her, slightly bowlegged.

18 April

Met Cleo – writing this while still fresh.

At the Chez Novak restaurant, where Pommier students go, the only seat left in the room when I walked in was opposite an attractive girl, obviously American, with a dark-brown ponytail. As the waiter patiently waited for her order she turned to me:

"I seem to be having trouble" and asked what pintadeau aux herbes was.

"Guinea hen. Chicken with personality."

She ordered the pintadeau and gave me a smile as reward. She explained that her French was not yet fluent. I asked if this was her first time at Chez Novak.

"Somebody mentioned it at Reid Hall."

"It's not the kind of place that would be listed in the Guide du Gourmand but according to the owner Mme Novak, her aim is to offer nourishing food at starving-artist prices."

"Do you always come here to eat?" she asked.

"Pretty much. She keeps the menu varied enough so you never get bored."

She had noticed that the room was crowded with as many old people as students.

"They're the neighborhood pensioners. Some of them go far back and remember Mme Novak from when she waited tables at Chez Rosalie and used to wait on Modigliani."

"Really? Modigliani?"

An accordionist appeared in the doorway and began

playing "Sous les cieux de Paris" with knotty fingers skittering in trills up and down the keyboard.

"So you're staying at Reid Hall."

"If you're a student at Smith and take your junior year in Paris you live at Reid Hall."

"Do you go to the Pommier?"

"No."

I asked her name.

"Cleo."

"Cleo the Queen of the Nile or is that Cleo with an i – Clio the muse of history?"

"Cleo with an e."

"Short for Cleopatra."

"Not short for anything. Just Cleo."

"How do you like it here?"

"Paris? I like it – of course. Who doesn't? but I intend living in Italy eventually – Florence – Rome – Venice. It doesn't really matter. Just Italy. The whole country's a museum."

Eating, I watch her discreetly. Between bites of the pintadeau she swivels her head to see herself in a narrow horizontal mirror running the length of one wall, narrowing her eyes in self-appraisal and grimacing. Her ponytail swirls languidly with her head movements. Then, reaching into a big leather handbag parked at her feet she takes out a pair of glasses, settles the wings behind her ears and reaches again into the bag and brings up a slim volume bound in fine apple-green linen. The book's title is in a handsome typeface stamped in gold: Les Fleurs du Mal."

"Baudelaire? In French?"

She laughed. "I'm not that good yet. In English."

The waiter came by and asked how she liked the

pintadeau.

"Ravissant," she said in a cheerful American voice.

I suggested coffee at Chez Patrick's. "The best coffee around."

"I have to get back."

"I'll walk you home, then."

"Do you know where Reid Hall is?"

At the street door she held out her hand.

"Establishment rules. Males not allowed above the ground floor."

"Do they do a bed check at ten?"

"It is a little old fashioned."

"How can you live in a place like this and enjoy Paris properly?"

"That, I think, is the idea – to enjoy Paris properly."

She didn't sound happy. I suggested she move to the Hotel Descartes on Rue Delambre. It had no rules about visitors or overnight stays.

"Do you know anybody who lives there?"

"A friend Jay lives there. Also a prostitute who hangs out at the Dôme lives there."

"You know a real prostitute?"

"She's very real. I'll introduce you."

"Honestly?"

"She likes artists. And she likes Americans, the great liberators."

I moved to kiss her but she pulled away.

"No," she said. "It leads to things."

"That's the idea."

"How about just saying goodnight?"

"Are you playing hard to get?"

"I'm not playing anything."

"Move out of here. To the Descartes."

But there was no use. I said I hoped we'd see each other again but the reality was I felt I was not in Paris but back in Jersey City again and I was hearing the old refrain: "I'm not that kind of girl."

Statues in Paris melted down by Nazis for munitions.

Maugham thought that the Quartier Montparnasse was "rather like Oxford." and I always wondered where he stood to get such an impression.

Le Sphinx: it was on Boulevard Edgar Quinet, a brothel said to be run by the Minister of the Interior.

In America, if before you get married you keep it in your pants, or in women's case panties, it means you have moral fiber. Which is the most important thing to have in life, moral fiber.

MORES (don't forget):

A TALE OF TWO BREASTS

I   At the Dôme. A braless girl at a café table. American businessman staring at her. Only the bottom button of the girl's short-sleeved shirt remains buttoned. It's a hot summer's day and the buttons left undone offer an unexpected glimpse of breast. While the businessman's wife chats with a friend at the table next to theirs, his eyes keep going back to the girl's shirt front and the girl, taking this in, discourages his look with a scowl. But the scowling doesn't work and now the situation calls for extreme measures. She gets to her feet and undoing the last button gives her shoulder an exaggerated swing and waggles her bare breasts at him.

"There – seen enough?"

II   In Paris biology and society coexist very happily. But in New York there's a war between them. A bare-breasted burlesque artist titillates men by flashing the tasselled nipples of a much-advertized pair of 48 DD breasts (insured by Lloyds of London for a million dollars a boob) by twirling them in circles in opposite directions. And that is okay. But a woman breastfeeding her baby in the park – that is not okay. Recently a woman seen giving her breast to her baby in an out-of-the-way corner of the park was jailed for thirty days for public indecency. The court ruled that her six-month-old baby be placed in a daycare facility run by nuns until the mother's release from jail. Early reports said that the baby did much crying at first but soon quieted down and became a "good baby".

19 April

Looking into Chez Patrick's this afternoon I saw her. From across the boulevard I watched her making the same odd faces in the mirror.

I crossed the boulevard and went in. It was strange meeting her like old friends. I suppose it's that she doesn't have many friends in Paris.

"Yes, that would be lovely," she said when I suggested a walk.

The day was sunnily warming up and perfect for a stroll through the Luxembourg Gardens. Chestnut trees made patches of light and shadow along the gravel paths. Two nannies on iron garden chairs chatted side by side as the children in their care played nearby.

Continuing past the puppet playhouse and the pony ride place we came out to the statues ringing the sailboat pond at the Boulevard St. Michel side. As we went past arched portes-cochères and stone passageways of ancient buildings I took her hand and felt the warmth of her fingers.

At Nôtre Dame we stopped at the bronze plaque in the pavement.

"All the distances in France are measured from this spot."

Further on we passed a drinking fountain, one of those for flâneurs that an Englishman named Wallace had given Paris as a gift.

On the Quai de Jemmapes, stopping for a rest on a bench alongside the tree-lined Canal St. Martin, we watched a scow piled high with sand sliding smoothly under the high arch of the iron footbridge. The Hôtel du Nord, where the film was shot, was on the other side of the canal.

Back in our neighborhood Cleo pointed to the outdoor urinal near the church at St. Germain des Prés and joked that women should be provided with similar conveniences. I told her of one of the models at the Pommier, Karin, the lesbian Norwegian, who confided using them at night, when nobody was around.

"Standing up?"

"On principle."

By the time we got back to her residence it was getting late. I put my arms around her, hugging her and taking in her body's fragrance and surprising freshness after all the walking. Then the familiar conversation: "Invite me up." / "Not allowed." / "How would they know?" / "They'd know." / "Move out." / "Can't."

I teased her. "Okay, here's the plan. We'd go at it hot and heavy and they'd come rushing into the room and catch us at flagrant – you know, whatever it is, flagrant whatever-o – and they'd ask you to leave, so you'd move right into the Hôtel Descartes, where they'd leave you alone. At the Descartes you could bring a zebra up to your room and nobody would care."

"Elephants too?" She was not to be swayed.

"They draw the line at elephants."

I moved to kiss her and hug that lovely body but she moved and the kiss turned into a collision of lips.

Result: insomnia. It was hard to get her out of my mind. My memory of her and my trouble sleeping that night as I thought of her, our walk together, the thought of women, all women, a woman's hug, the gorgeous, soft-skinned, sweet-smelling half of the human race, their faces, voices, their bodies, the movement of their thighs when they walk, their hippy movement when they run, their breasts, their hair, their manner of talking, the way they view life, their emotional intensity . . .

20 April

I try to practice my French on Mme Verger but she beats me to the punch and practices her English on me. Meeting in the hallway she pipes up:

"You are 'appy 'ere?"

"Oh yes," I reply, "I am 'appy 'ere."

A you-have-made-my-day grin as she floats by. Is that gin I smell?

Justin, making my bed: "Do you ever paint nudes?"

"That's all we do at the Pommier."

"Because there's always a market for nudes. People enjoy looking at nude women. You know?"

21 April

Many wartime shortages still – especially coal and some imported fruits but electricity the most difficult shortage to get used to. The government, to conserve energy, turns electric power off for a few hours a day, so that as you look in the mirror and examine the jaw that you're shaving the room creepily goes dark. Hours later power turns on again, silently.

31

Later

My French has a long way to go but Mme Verger's English shows hope.

"Each year we put on the black clothing attend memorial beeg event Place de la Concorde, where outrage committed, yes? Guillotine the good king Louis Seize."

Apparently a group of hard-core royalists troop reverently to the Place des Pyramides, the other hallowed ground. It was there, in 1429, that a brave young virgin fell fighting an "army of English hoodlums."

Monsieur Verger tells how during the Reign of Terror a Mme Tallien did a lot of bed-hopping. She saved many a man from the guillotine by granting her favors to certain administrators.

(Hein?).

I learned from them two interesting facts about the French Revolution not taught in American schools: (a) This Mme Tallien was said to take baths in the juice of strawberries for their healing properties and (b) she often skipped wearing underwear. I suppose the argument would be why put something on just to take it off?

I tried to imagine sharing a bed with somebody strawberry-flavored.

The Vergers and Justin are educating me. That's how they view it. In a sense they are.

A newspaper this morning verbally slammed a minister, saying he was a connard. I looked it up. The word means bugger or jackass. And a colleague of his was a salaud – no, he was the extreme of salaud, a salaud fini, the fini implying the son of a bitch had at his core some quintessential refinement of rottenness. He was the finished article, splendid in moral decay.

"He's a couille molle."

I had to look that one up too: "couille molle – mushy testicle." A fine example of French political analysis.

The Vergers attempt to correct any views I might have picked up on modern European history, by which they mean modern French history. They're teaching me the importance of restoring the monarchy to France. Their purpose, I think, is to counterbalance any egalitarian drivel I may have acquired in America, a country where citizens are brainwashed into conforming little idiots. Present company excluded, of course.

The valet Justin, though a royalist, feels the poor need the Fourteenth of July. It pacifies them, calms them down. It stops them from being crazed into a regicidal mob. Some such reasoning. Speaking this way elevates him to eloquence. He says that appeasing a crowd renders it impuissant against society's stabilizing force, the royalists (!), on whom all progress depends.

For the Vergers, the Fourteenth of July is a day of mourning. I have the feeling that Madame's and Monsieur's politics are what keep them going until the day that the unworkability of socialism is finally understood even by the poor imbeciles who believe in it. And as for communism, don't make them puke.

Mme Verger drinks. By evening she's soused. It's definitely gin.

The one thing Monsieur Verger and I agree on is the guillotine. I find it painful to think of a human being bending his neck down on a block of wood so that another human being can slice his head off.

22 April

Thanks to the GI Bill I'm learning what painters do – which is mostly quite a nuisance, or some of it is anyway. At "my" Colarossi studio I dunk the brushes in turpentine to soak off most of the oil paint. Then lather the bristles against a big brown cake of laundry soap in the old black-and-urine-colored sink that looks like it hasn't been operational since the 1920s. Rinsing the brushes under the rusty tap water dribbling from the old-fashioned brass faucet is tedious work. I spread the brushes on the old wooden floorboards to dry.

Late afternoon I arrange a still-life of two still-green bananas, a plump aubergine and a black-handled paring knife against a white cloth. When I go back in the morning all that's left are dried purple-green slivers of aubergine peels and half of one of the bananas sticking partway out of a smooth-edged hole in the floorboards where the rats had had trouble pulling it through. With my shoe I squish the remainder of the banana through the smooth-edged hole and decide never to paint anything edible, not there. The paring knife is gone and I wonder if the rats are trying to work out things to do with it.

I'm in La Bohème, an artist in Montparnasse.

I told Cleo about Colarossi and she asked if it was a real artist's studio and could she see it.

"It's real, all right. It even has a model's platform. And good light," I said.

"Have you ever thought of sharing it?"

"Come and have a look."

I explain how to get there.

The next day as I work I hear a commotion in the yard. From the big studio windows I see Cleo in the courtyard, arms loaded with what looks like painter's equipment. Then a noisy clatter up the stairs and Cleo's cheerful face in the doorway.

"You sure it's all right?" she says with an overly sweet voice but marches right in without my superfluous assurance that she's welcome.

Looking bright, she traipses across the studio lugging a folding easel, a paint box, a palette with dried color splotches, a paint-stained smock, a large glass jar crammed with brushes, a half-finished canvas, a portable radio trailing an improvised picture-wire antenna. Carefully placing everything on the floor against the far wall – to demonstrate, I think, how small a space she would be occupying and definitely not getting in my way. She turns to me with a questioning look for final authorization.

"Half the studio is yours," I say to encourage her. "There's loads of room to spread out if you want." I just want her there.

"Incredible space," she says in genuine awe as she looks around. "How did you get this place?"

I explain that never having seen anyone enter or leave, it looked uninhabited. So one day I climbed up for a look and saw this enormous empty studio, large enough for "Guernica" and well lit from a north-facing wall that from waist up was all windows and I just squatted. I keep expecting to be thrown out at some point but so far no one has questioned my being there.

She carefully sets up her easel and places a half-finished canvas on it. I'm surprised to see a still-life of dappled red-and-green apples as solid-looking as the real Normandy fruit. It's not amateur painting but conscientious, disciplined work. For a moment I feel bad about what I'm doing. I am of course a fraud – a painter only because of the GI Bill.

With her things set up she begins working immediately while I secretly observe her close up. I feel a happiness, as though I were being let in on something. She squints at the canvas and after a swift appraisal applies a dab of red on one of the apples before taking several steps backwards. Another squint and a brisk march forward to place a dab of yellow-green to one of the other apples. Retreat and squint, advance and dab, retreat and squint – all at once I become aware she's observing me observing her and she stops.

35

"Sorry," I say. "I hope I'm not disturbing you."

"That's OK," she says with charming insincerity.

First asking and making sure I would not mind if she turned on the radio, she tunes in to a classical music station and turns the sound low. Bach's Magnificat.

"Do you like Bach?"

Yes of course and I'm thinking: quiet days in Montparnasse, windows open, balmy afternoons – life.

"Me too. I love Bach," she says and turns the radio louder and continues painting.

I feel happy just having her there.

She hates Hemingway. He's a "he-man macho alcoholic bully." She barely cares that he once had a flat not far from here, Pound too, and before them Strindberg and Whistler. So many – Sargent, de Chirico, Leger – all living in these same two or three streets ("one of the great things about Paris," I interject).

I learn more about her. She tells me about her background as an adopted orphan, her adoptive parents a Connecticut couple. We try guessing Cleo's ethnic roots. She doubts even her foster parents know. Judging by her looks we make guesses at her origins: Swedish . . . Danish . . . Icelandic . . . anyway, Scandinavian.

"Whatever," she says and adds she doesn't think she's that good looking, meaning Scandinavian.

She laughs when I ask if orphans feel unhappy or in some way disconnected with the world, and she says she feels very happy and totally connected with her adoptive parents. They're her real parents. She has never known any other. She wouldn't know how an orphan feels. Only one thing in life makes her unhappy and that's her bottom.

"Your bottom?" I pretend to take an interested look at it.

"It's rather a nice ass," I assure her.

She takes that in. Wheels go round.

"The English call it a bum – so much nicer than a-a-ass. Brief, succinct – bum."

I tell her she has not only a brief, succinct bum but a sexy one and if we had a tape measure we could measure it if that would reassure her. "And while we're at it have a look at your pudenda." A silly joke but making the humor broad so as not to inadvertently offend.

"At my what?"

Batting her eyes, glaring at me. But fighting a smile.

23 April

Fact file. In French there's no word for pickup, meaning a woman casually met at a bar or on the street. The closest the dictionary comes is partenaire de rencontre – encounter partner. In borrowing the English word, the French give it an altogether different meaning. In French "pickup" means record player.

24 April

Spring days, nicely warming. The local prostitute Yette – short for Henriette. She calls out to me as I pass the Dôme on my way to the Pommier. We've become friends. She long ago mapped out her streetwalking territory: the mostly-empty stretch of Boulevard Montparnasse from the cluster of cafes at Vavin all the way down to the Gare Montparnasse. Working nights and putting in late hours she gets out of bed around noon and I bump into her now as she is having her morning wake-up coffee.

Surprisingly Yette believes in love. She assures me nothing is more important in life. So much, she says, for all the bullshit you hear about prostitutes being cynical about love.

Sipping her morning café au lait she reflects: "Sounds like sentimental crap coming from a whore (une pute, she frankly calls herself) but you'll see, it's true. But you have to live a while first. Without love you have nothing. And if you have love you have everything."

She likes talking about love. I think she must once have been in love, she talks about it so much.

She asks me now, "And you, what do you know about love?"

"Only the love affairs in books. I've never been in love."

"You don't know what you're missing."

The next time Yette and I bump into each other it's at the Dôme. Early evening, the sky clouding over. Across the boulevard the whitish-green bronze of Rodin's Balzac, the deep-socketed eyes gazing out at Paris – or Montparnasse anyway.

She joins me and orders a hot wine. The oyster vendor is working in his separate plastic-covered space surrounded by bushel baskets of moist green-and-brown seaweed that nestles spiny sea urchins and black mussels. Warmed by a charcoal brazier the vendor knifes open fresh oysters and as we watch, a woman, head bent under the falling rain, ducks into his plastic enclosure and buys a dozen unopened flat grey Marennes and a dozen turquoise Portugaises.

People arrive chatting, noisily drifting among the tables. I ask Yette how things are going. So-so she says.

Usually she sits alone to attract a client. Police regulations prohibit prostitutes from soliciting clients on commercial premises. At a cafe, for example, they are permitted to speak to you only if you speak to them first. Otherwise it's soliciting.

Somewhere inside me I'm still in Jersey City and I find it exciting to meet a woman who is quite frankly a prostitute – and accepts me as a friend. She speaks of her work as "skilled labor". She's humorous about it.

I find it hard to imagine having sex with someone of her girth. Before the war, her figure had been svelte, she says. She had worked in a brothel in Deauville, a fairly posh maison close called Le Phare. When the Nazis overran France they took over Le Phare as a Wehrmacht officer's club and then after the war the locals took their revenge at what they saw as treason by running Yette and the other women out of town. I had seen the newsreels. The women were stripped naked on the street and had their heads shaved as the respectable women of the town jeered at them. They even shaved the head of the middle-aged chamber maid even though she had only cooked and changed the linens. She too had given aid and comfort to the enemy and all had provided services in "horizontal collaboration".

Yette ended up as a street prostitute working the Montparnasse area, where she let herself go and put on a massive amount of weight. She had been getting plump over the years and now as she grew stout and then enormous only a very few men wanted her. But fortunately there are men who like their women big.

"Probably poor idiots in need of maternal solace, right? You meet all kinds."

Her one complaint is that her breasts have become so

monstrueux they have to be supported by expensive custom-made brassieres.

"They're watermelons," she said.

Her preferred café in Montparnasse is the Dôme, never the Rotonde. The Coupole is good too but mostly for tea and dancing. The Dôme is the only real café.

Her talk of love surprises me but everything about Yette surprises me, most of all her monumental weight: close to a hundred and fifty kilos. She has the shape of a Wagnerian soprano, one of those big-barreled pigtailed Tyrolean Isoldes that most Tristans can barely get both arms around. When she laughs her body shakes all over – she quivers. She calls her body weight her tonnage.

Nevertheless she attracts clients and even has repeat visits, one a married businessman up from Bordeaux twice a month who takes her out to the Bois for dinner and a weekend of looking at the paintings in the Orangerie or the Rodin Museum at Meudon.

"A real gentleman."

He likes what she has, her marchandise.

"He likes his women big. He'd leave his wife but she's a Catholic and would kill herself if he left, if you can believe that. His wife, a devout Catholic, would commit suicide, right? But he's a gentleman and likes me for my knockers and takes me out to dinner and I know a lot of men who wouldn't give you even that. Une baise, a quick fuck is all they want, and then, allez, oup!"

Men are to Yette as puss-ihhh is to Jay. She likes men, likes talking with them. But she assures me they're all pretty much bastards. Then a quick glance not quite in my direction:

"Most men."

Friday, 25 April

I keep thinking of Stendhal but even with him as spiritual guide, my progress, handicapped by Jersey City mores in man-woman relations, followed nineteenth- or eighteenth-century rules of courtship. When the directrice of a gallery on Rue la Boétie contacted her royalist friend Mme Verger to arrange for someone young and artistically inclined to give her private lessons in English, Mme Verger asked if I'd be interested. As a dollar-a-lesson supplement to my $75 a month just to chat in English with a Frenchwoman – and who knows what that might lead to? – I jumped at it.

The directrice looked a little on the older side: around thirty-five, at a guess. She had brown eyes and dark brown hair and was a bandbox picture: black velvet skirt, white blouse, black velvet jacket.

She led the way behind the gallery's display area to her office, a cozy alcove with a comfy-looking couch and a fur rug on which a long-haired black-and-white cat lay sprawled, erupting, on seeing her, into a raucous purring. The directrice picked up the cat ("Mallarmé") and stroked it while cradling it in her lap, explaining in a friendly voice that this was merely a get-acquainted visit and encouraged me to drop in any time I wanted to give her a lesson. With a charming eye-contacting smile she said she was often in the mood and told me we could start as early as the next day. At the moment she was expecting an important collectioneur, but tomorrow, when she would have more time, we would be undisturbed and happy there. Another warm smile.

I took her to be referring to the snug sitting arrangement and felt the interpretation confirmed when I showed up the next day and she led me directly to the alcove and thigh-touchingly sat beside me on the couch. Wearing a perfume that made me dream, she seemed eager to learn. I liked the easy intimacy of her friendship and felt that with the way things were going and her impatience to get to work, her English would improve rapidly.

As the cat with the outboard motor leaped to her lap, I took out our textbook, Shaw's prefaces. We began working on English pronunciation, tackling first the th sound and then devoting some of the lesson to restraining "how it works" from becoming "owee twerks" and "do it at once" from

41

sliding into "do ee taa-twahnce". (She had, she told me, a friend living in the U.K. in a place called Press-TWEEK.)

I tried to make the lesson sound interesting, but the séance did not appear to proceed well, and seeing her discouraged look as I left, I concluded I was demanding too much of her and needed to push less hard. But when I got back to my hotel, the propriétaire, Mme Verger, informed me that her gallery directrice friend had just phoned to say she had suddenly been called away to Lawndruh and wouldn't be back for a month and quite possibly longer and to be sure to thank me for my lesson. "Hein?" – Mme Verger here giving me a conspiratorial smile.

Saturday, 26 April

Woke up this morning with that same feeling of renewed happiness at being in Paris and just as I got out of bed and started shaving I heard a discreet knock at the door: Mme Verger. Could she step in for a moment? A man's glove was found on the stairs and she asks if by any chance it might be mine. I don't own gloves. Ah. There being no chair in the room I offer her the as-yet unmade bed as a place to sit. She genteelly lowers her slim posterior to the bed as close as possible to the edge without sliding off. She comments that the sheet is still warm and as she smoothes her tweed skirt against her sleek thighs, she laughs at the socially risqué implications. She thanks me for letting her catch her breath and as we exhaust our small talk she rises to her feet, regarding me head-tiltingly, and with a nervous smile, not quite looking at me, whispers goodbye. I later tell Jay about her early-morning visit and he says: "To my knowledge, that makes you the first resident of the hotel that Madame hasn't boffed. Yet."

"What do you mean?"

"She was obviously hoping you'd boff her."

"Boff her?"

"Give her a shag, a bang."

She did not seem like someone who banged. Seriously? Madame Verger the royalist bangs? "She's my landlady."

"Between the sheets everybody is a commoner, even landladies. And as a commoner, she does what commoners do in bed."

"What's that?"

"She fucking bangs."

Jay smiles and looks at me pityingly, a source of amusement to him.

"The army didn't do you much good, did it?"

Monday, 28 April

Out of the blue, a letter from home, my mother wanting to know about my daily life "complete with details" – describing it as "the flavor of Paris." How I'm doing, who I'm meeting, what I'm eating, how the weather is. Desperate for something to write about, I describe my friend Yette and her "tonnage", thinking that with my mother's perennially dieting it might cheer her up to know there's someone in Paris who outweighs her by a considerable margin. I take the precaution of lying that she's one of the models at the Pommier. To avoid cardiac arrest.

Tuesday, 29 April

Monsieur and Madame ask if I'd like to accompany them to a Joan of Arc ceremony in an anniversary of some sort. "Franch heestory," Monsieur encourages me in his best English. With regret I tell them of a conflict in schedule and later tell Yette about the invitation. She surprises me with the intensity of her anger.

"What do you want to do with royalists – with morons? Why do you want to hang out with idiots?"

I explain I don't hang out with idiots. It's their hotel and I can't exactly avoid them.

This is not the time to tell her I think they're likable idiots. I don't give a damn that they're crazy royalists.

Saturday, 3 May

The latest in the Cleo saga. Learning how tight a budget Cleo lives on I invited her to lunch yesterday at the Restaurant du Pont. Its specialité is bifteck à cheval. The cheval refers not to horsemeat but to a fried egg sitting on the steak sunnyside up, like a saddle.

We had just begun the meal with bread chunks and raw radishes and butter when the server of our table, a tall country girl with a boxer's biceps, guffawed and pointed toward the windows. With a concerned look, the proprietor swiftly emerged from behind his comptoir to see what for-god-sake had got into his server. Diners around the room, forks lifted halfway to mouths, put them down again and twisted in their seats to look at the narrow street filling with students from the Écoles des Beaux Arts. Students jammed three and four deep around a float of a monumental, five-storey-high papiermâché human cock. You wouldn't call it a penis: it was a cock – a hardon. Nestled at the base of the enormous pink and red totemic erection was a pair of orange balls the size of first-prize-winning county-fair pumpkins, each a couple of meters in diameter. The massive plum-shaped purple knob at the top of the heroic hardon was at eye level with the top storeys of the buildings, and as the students chanted obscene ditties, the smiling housewives hanging out of upper-storey windows shouted down to the students "In your dreams!" One woman yelled to the other women, "No, in our dreams."

It signaled the opening of the twenty-four-hour Quat'z'Arts ball, the annual art students' festival-cum-orgy that in moral license made the New Orleans Mardi Gras look like a church picnic. Cleo and I gulped down our meal to follow the spectacle as the stately totem moved with quivering majesty through the quartier St. Germain, past the Deux Magots, the Flore and the Brasserie Lipp, where the sidewalk diners applauded the procession lumbering past their tables. People queuing at the bus stop at the Église St. Germain laughed at the hardon as the crowd oozed toward Boulevard St. Michel past smiling agents de police busily squeezing cars and inquisitive pedestrians to one side of the boulevard to ease the great dong's progress.

Cleo, eyes flashing, took in two nuns coming out of the Église and nudged my elbow. The attractive-looking younger of the two nuns glanced at the mammoth erection before casting her eyes down.

"Touching, isn't it?" I said, seeing the shyness of the young nun. "Poor woman."

"Regrets, you think?"

"Or fond memories. Maybe regrets too."

Monday, 5 May

In my mailbox a rejection of "Parisian Prostitute" from the "Left Bank Review". My piece on Yette.

. . .

AFTERNOON OF A PUTE

Yette at the Dôme, She's installed at her place on the terrasse well inside the glass enclosure put up against the late autumn and winter weather. She says she worries about me, always seeing me without a petite amie. She sounds lonely to me and looking for someone to talk with, and feel this confirmed when she growls: "Sit down!"

"Aren't you looking to get married some day?" she asks.

Marriage is too far in the future even to think about.

"The Dôme's not the place to look for a wife," she adds.

I ask what she means.

"You kidding? You won't find a wife at the Dôme." She laughs at the thought. "Unless, of course, it's somebody else's wife."

A rain starts outside the enclosure. Blurry yellow and green neons in the shop windows light the boulevard. The wet pavement gives off a pleasantly acrid smell.

One of the filles operating from the Dôme comes walking back from the Gare, eying the terrace as she approaches and ducks in out of the rain.

"On the streets, rainy nights are the hardest," Yette says, taking in the girl. "Working in a brothel spoils you."

The fille takes a small table near a GI painter I recognize from the Pommier, glancing frequently at him. She's hoping he'll notice and speak to her.

Yette thinks the GIs are sympas. They are men who don't slap women around and always buy them drinks even when they're broke. They just run up a tab and pay at the beginning of the next month.

I pump her for information about the women who worked with her when she was a madam in Deauville. One of the girls, she said, had retired to a monastery and worked for a parish priest who protected adolescent girls from being tricked into prostitution by pimps. One bought a tobacco shop near Lille. Another married a deputy mayor of a village where no one knew of her past.

"How did it work out?"

"It worked out well. He was a kind mayor and she made a good wife. And a very faithful one too."

A couple of her girls either turned lesbian or had been lesbian all along. Probably the latter, she thought.

"All prostitutes are a little bi. Some of them turn that way living together."

I asked her about S&M and the various things prostitutes are sometimes asked to do – the things you read about in books.

"What is this, an interview?"

"I'm just curious."

"Your eyes are like saucers." She smiled benevolently and said she was just an old whore now. "But others have it worse than me."

I asked her if she did anything a client asked.

"Like what?"

"Like anything. Whatever."

"You're interviewing me, all right. For S&M I refer clients to my colleague Georgette."

"She likes S&M?"

"She keeps whips and leather and pretends the client is her former husband. She's very funny about it. Her former husband's a pimp."

Pimps are crapules. They raid Montparnasse to add women to their labor force. And cops too – les flics. The two sometimes work as a team. First the cops harassed you for a little rake-off and made life difficult. Then one day a pimp comes along and says don't worry, he'll talk to the species of cons, and presto, the cops stop harassing you. But now you belong to the pimp.

"The underworld. An interesting place. Corrupt as hell." She had no use for any of them.

Pimps and flics always reach a cozy arrangement. The pimp gives the flics a weekly cadeau of a few thousand francs, and the flics give his women protection, and everybody is happy – everybody, that is, except the women.

Yette launched into a story about a repeat client, a senator she's been seeing for two years who likes a good spanking. She says his ass is so sore he can barely sit anymore. Some like to be led around the room on a leash. Or pretend she's the mistress of the house scolding them, the timid butler, for daring to touch Madame there! For shame! Some men want a quick baise just after another man has finished and before she has washed, and experienced filles knew the trick of applying a mix of watery flour paste and a drop of bleach.

"Men don't want women. They want their fantasies of women." Pointing a thumb at her massive body: "Can you imagine somebody asking me to pretend I was a young schoolgirl in pigtails?"

I had heard of the Guide Rose, which was like a Michelin guide but for houses of prostitution. I asked her if she had ever contributed to it.

"No, books like that are written by the experts."

"Like who? Who are the experts?"

"Like the cops." She laughed.

"Do they – "

"Hey! Stop interviewing me."

"It's just that I'm curious."

"Just try relaxing."

I looked around at the evening crowd. Groups of people were arriving, couples mostly. A chatty woman with two men came in. Yette turned to me:

"Americans."

"By the way they're dressed?"

"By the way they rush around. Even if they're just going to a café for a drink you'd think they were late for an appointment."

We talked some more and she taught me "chaude pisse", which means the clap, and a few other expressions I might find useful in life, she said. And her favorite expletive, putain! saying it in an angry voice, which was amusing coming from her. Putain means whore.

I asked if she had American clients.

"Ah," she said, "the interview goes on. You never give up. No, my clients are mostly just the men of the quarter. A husband might tell his wife he feels a need to stretch his legs after dinner, and an hour later, feeling much better, he goes home to a nice scene of domestic harmony."

She explained that that was less complicated than sneaking off for a few hours a week to see a lover and posed less of a threat than the potential exposure of an affair. It was all as a harmless supplement to matrimony and actually a protector of marital love. This did not make her cynical about marriage – not at all. Of course she herself wouldn't marry most men if you paid her, not after what she knew about them. She liked her arrangement with the Bordeaux industrialist just as she liked her freedom. One had to be realistic about the glandular differences between males and females and recognize the age-old need in men for change.

"Toujours perdrix," she said. "Do you understand?"

"Always partridge. Meaning?"

"Champagne gets boring if you have it for breakfast, lunch and dinner. And if the whole truth were known, women too enjoy variety and can be as clever as cats in heat in finding ways to compensate for any indifference or neglect at home. So let the husband beware. All those stupid jokes about cuckolds are not fairy tales."

I asked her about something that had puzzled me. At dusk at a certain corner on the Rue de Rivoli, near Concorde, I had noticed nicely dressed teenage girls. Yette knew where I meant and said a social convention was involved. In the early evening a girl of seventeen or eighteen would go there looking for some fatherly gentleman who knew the rules of the game, and if they both hit it off, he would invite her to a restaurant and afterwards, if they found pleasure in each other's company, they would end the evening in a comfortable hotel.

"Comme ça, everybody's happy."

"Cozy."

"Safe too."

I asked her some more questions about herself.

"Ah merde, more interview."

"Sorry. I won't ask any more."

"Oh-h," she sounded remorseful. "I don't really mind. Shoot."

"I only wanted to know how many men you'd had in your life. I guess that sounds pretty indiscreet."

"Fucked for money? A thousand, maybe two thousand. Not many."

"Have you ever been a poule de luxe?"

She laughed. "With my tonnage?"

Poules de luxe are modern courtesans with expensive jewels and clothing and engaged by the week, month, sometimes even by the season by the châteaux-ed aristocracy in stadium-size apartments in the beaux quartiers. They command astronomical fees.

"Their clientele are Saudi oil princes with private jets. They fly out a dozen or two courtesans to Riyadh for a week of fun behind palace walls."

"I heard that a lot of Englishmen come down to Paris for a weekend of sex."

"The English don't have sex."

"What do you mean?"

She was critical of Anglo-Saxons and laughed.

"Only Anglo-Saxons say (mimicking an Englishwoman): 'Oh, I have just eaten – oh, I cannot make love now.' Which of course is idiotic. After lunch is a very good time to make love."

"When's a bad time to make love?"

She laughed again. What a ridiculous question. "There is no bad time to make love. And there is no best time either. It's always a good time. Whenever you both feel like it – that's the best time."

"Is there a best way?"

"Of course there's a best way. Avec tendresse. What a question."

She told me some Frenchwomen didn't mind if their husband was unfaithful to them when he was away on business. Certainly not if he was gone for a month. That way, when he came back, he would still be en forme. Any sexual experiences the husband might have had while away did not count. You didn't keep a ledger about these things.

"If he strayed just once it was for practice," she added as an afterthought.

She sounded like she genuinely believed that.

"And besides," she said, "what the wife doesn't know wouldn't hurt her."

I asked her if in Paris infidelity was as common as people believed it was. Or was that just a stereotype?

"Why only Paris? It happens in all of France. And it's no stereotype. With some people it's going to happen anyway, so why not accept it instead of making such a big fuss over it?"

I expressed surprise at such easy attitudes and asked her how she felt about them.

"It's quite normal, I think, given human nature."

"Would you like it if it happened to you?"

"Well, if it happened I wouldn't be able to stop it, would I?"

"But would you like it?"

"It's not a bad arrangement if it suits the two of them, is it?"

"Yes, but would you like it?"

"Oh, you know, in life you get accustomed to everything."

As a teenager Yette had wanted to be an artist and knew quite a bit of art history. It was from her that I first heard that when a wealthy collector had tried to donate his collection of Pissarros, Monets and Sisleys to the national museum it caused a scandal among critics. They said the paintings were a heap of excrement. They would dishonor French art.

"That's the story of art. But now they all hang in a national museum, hein?"

I was always surprised by the things she knew.

"So," she went on, "the Americans started buying them

and ever since then the French have complained that Americans come over here and buy up their French art and leave them with nothing. They start pitying themselves. And it's these same idiots, you know, who called the Balzac over there – see that wonderful piece of sculpture across the boulevard? – they called it a sack of flour with a head stuck on top! Can you imagine? I'm not exaggerating. This is all true. And as for Toulouse-Lautrec, he was dismissed as a low-lifer. His friends called him Teapot Toulouse because he had a short body but a huge schwanz. You know what a schwanz is?"

"Is it his – you know, his . . .?"

"Exactly. His cock."

"Is that your description?"

"Mine, no. How would I know? The girls who knew him described it that way. It must have been quite a spout. They called him a prick on wheels, he liked fucking so much. They don't teach you that in art classes. Who's your favorite painter?"

"I don't know. Picasso occasionally, sometimes. Matisse."

She said she likes the Impressionists, although Picasso is good and Matisse – well, it depends on which period. But he's a good colorist. Am I familiar with the work of Marquet?

Her interest impresses me. She says I'd like Marquet and Utrillo too, although Utrillo is considered low taste. But she doesn't think so at all.

She finishes her coffee and begins to get up and instantly changes her mind and plops all her weight down again. "Business is slow this time of day. But if I go home I'll fall asleep and I've already slept too much today."

"Maybe somebody will come along."

"I doubt it. I get most of my business between five and seven."

"Why then?"

"Husbands. Going home from work."

53

She reminds me that if I should ever need help with French she would be glad to teach me. So I ask her about a phrase I keep hearing. It's a dazzling defiance of syntax: "Ah non, mais ça alors, vous savez, hein?" It's spoken angrily, in a confrontational tone, and the whole thing comes out as a single blistering multisyllabic word. From context I think it means "Just what the hell do you think you're doing?" But if you take the words by themselves the question seems devoid of meaning: "Ah no, but that then, you know, huh?" I wrote it down to memorize it for possible use some day to see if I could pass myself off as a native but so far an opportunity has never come up. Even in its shortened form, "Non, mais!" I could never squeeze it into a conversation.

I tell Yette: "Actually I did try out the abbreviated form once, but it lacked conviction."

She laughs. "You have to say the words with outrage or you will never be mistaken for a Frenchman."

She helps me with common phrases like "belle époque". It means beautiful age, or wonderful period of history. The trouble is I've heard it so many times describing so many different periods of history that I can never pin down when exactly that beautiful age occurred.

"The problem is," Yette explains, "there have been several of them. Between the wars, in the twenties and thirties, that was considered la belle époque, but others say, no no, the real belle époque was 1914. Purists of course insist that the true belle époque was the period before the First World War, around 1900. But others argue that the Gay Nineties was la grande époque."

"It has no absolute meaning, then."

"No."

"So when Giacometti arrived in Paris in 1922 and declared that Montparnasse was dead, it was no longer the belle époque."

"There you go."

"It just means the past is always better than the present."

"Au bon vieux temps."

"The good old days."

"Arcadie. How would you say Arcadie in English?"

"Arcadia."

"Voilà."

Keeping an eye down the boulevard she says:

"OK, no more interviewing. Interview over."

Cuffing my arm with one hand she said "Let's go" and with the other signaled the waiter for the bill. And insisted on paying for me.

"Students are always broke, so shut up. We're going for some moules. I invite you. But no more interviews."

She led the way to a bistro around the corner. It was a small popular place and on some nights you couldn't get a table. We lucked out. There was a free table way in the back of the small room just near the kitchen. From where we sat we could see chefs cooking. One of them smiled at Yette and over the noise of the kitchen mouthed the word bonjour.

When the waiter came over Yette waved away the menu card and ordered the house specialty, moules marinières. From where we were sitting we could watch its preparation. Yette said they always had mussels fresh in from the Breton coast. The muscles were splashed with white wine and steamed open in their own juice, which was flavored with sautéed minced onions and shallots. I was fascinated watching the preparation. Black pepper, bay leaf, thyme, a handful of chopped parsley. The waiter brought it to us in a gallon aluminum pot and set the pot on the table. The broth tasted of sea air. After we had each eaten two dozens of the indigo-black mussels and washed them down with a bottle of Pouilly-Fuissé, carefully pyramiding the empty shells on our plates, we used pieces of baguette to mop up the juice and onion bits at the pot's shiny bottom.

Yette, never reserved to begin with, became even less inhibited after a few warming wines, and her cheerful Burgundian features, the kind Renoir enjoyed painting, reminded me of the stories of the middle-aged Kiki, the former model and once belle et scandaleuse "Queen of Montparnasse", arriving at the Dôme amiably smashed from refueling stops along the way. Hiking her skirts to mid-thigh she cancanned past amused early-Saturday-evening people on the boulevard and toward friends on the Dôme's terrace applauding her arrival. There were many Kiki stories about her hating to wear underclothing and getting thrown out of the Bal Bullier after a dance on a table gave the audience the uncensored version of the cancan, the whole thrill of which was the absence of underwear. Yette had some of the same spirit but of course was far heavier than Kiki, even Kiki in middle age, but her face had a certain Kiki look through a Burgundian resemblance. Kiki once said "I was well-fucked last night" while contentedly ordering brioche and café au lait at the Dôme the next morning, and Yette had the same unheld-back Parnassian style. I really loved her and it wasn't the wine speaking.

On our second bottle of Pouilly-Fuissé, I could see her feeling carefree and slipping into prankish mode and I felt happy for her. Chatting winefully over a second pot of moules, she selected an unusually fat mussel and splayed it open to show its fleshy meat edged with black mussel shell and stringy beard at the top and lowered it to her lap saying, or rather bubbling privately to herself, body jiggling, "That's pretty much it up close." And then it was an after-dinner brandy, following which the two of us looking like the world's unlikeliest couple headed out the door for a post-brandial brandy at the Dôme, Yette happily leading the way with a hand stealthily groping behind her in a friendly search of my balls to give them a tweak of playful sociability and neighborly affection.

Tuesday, 6 May

Yette piece back. Wasted no time rejecting it. This time from the new Swiss Three Peaks Revue. It joins three other rejects recently, never any reasons given, just stock replies:

"Thank you for your recent submission, which we have considered with care. I fear that we do not feel able to offer you the representation you seek."

"We're sorry to say that this piece wasn't right for us, despite its evident merit. Thank you for allowing us to consider your work, and we sincerely apologize for the delay in responding."

"It is the policy of this agency not to . . ."

". . . despite its evident merit. Thank you for allowing us to consider your work."

"Thank you for sending . . . fiction market growing increasingly difficult . . . we are very sorry we . . ."

Wednesday, 7 May

Sandrine posing again at the Pommier and showing no hard feelings. She shoots me a secret smile as students concentrate on their canvases and sketch pads. The session over, she's dressed and gone before I can fold away my easel and go over to her. I have a strange thought seeing her leave: am I, however slightly, in love with her? Not love – affection? A little, if I had to give it a name. Felt sad seeing her slipping away quickly.

Thursday, 8 May

Last night invited Cleo to the cinema in that little street, Jules Chaplain. GIs from the Pommier there in surprising force. Some go for the publicité, little one-minute filmed commercials, a particular favorite, a commercial for a shampoo called Dop. It shows a woman standing in a pond in water up to her shoulders and lathering her hair and then the moment the GIs wait for: the rinsing off. To wash the soap from her head she falls backward in a plunge that for a half-second flashes her pubic hair as her nude torso sinks into the water and a hysterical male voiceover simultaneously screams, "Dop! Dop! DOP!" It took just two viewings for the GIs to pick up the cue and join the voiceover in a loud chorus of "Dop! Dop! DOP!" demonstrating, I suppose, the hoped-for power of advertising, though not in the way intended, because nobody I knew ever went out and bought any DOP or even remembered it was a shampoo.

As I walk her back to her place, she thanks me for the evening, loving in particular the running GI commentary during the talkier love scenes, as when Jean Gabin persists in lovey-dovey banter with Danielle Darrieux, and an American voice calls out in the dark auditorium: "Fuck her, man, she's begging you!" The ever-courteous Cleo loves the "so much greater freedom here than in Northampton."

Friday, 9 May

For me all of life is nothing more than my experience of life. A truism and I made the mistake of telling it to Cleo, with the comment:

"It's original."

"By original you mean banal."

Saturday, 10 May

Getting nowhere with Cleo. She's heard of a lesbian nightclub called Le Monocle, offering women dancing partners. She asks if I'd like to go.

I know of the place and had been there once. Men are not discouraged at Le Monocle but it's mostly a place of entertainment for women. It sounds like she would like to go. She heads me off: no.

"Have you ever danced with a lesbian?" she asks.

"Not knowingly. I'm sure it would be a mixed pleasure. For her and for me."

A friend at the Pommier had described it as a dikey hangout so one rainy evening I had gone out of curiosity and found the small dark dance floor empty except for a woman in her fifties, at a guess. A shocking age in a dance partner for someone only twenty-one, but okay, what the hell, and Amazonian in build, also okay, and with a baritone voice and wearing a swallow-tail tuxedo, that too, I suppose, okay, but her resemblance to Winston Churchill was not so okay even after she removed her cigar with the hand that gripped my back to smash me to her bosom for a quick cheek-to-cheek spin around the empty dance floor.

"I like you," she said, after planting the cigar back in her mouth.

I fled.

Cleo's reaction: "You're afraid of women. Men so often seem to be."

"Afraid of women!"

"Lesbians are women too. You're afraid of a lesbian."

Debating now whether to try another essay, this one on the Toilets of Paris. A weirdo idea but maybe publishable. The Genteel Art, no, The Gentle Art of Making Peepee – some cutesy title like that. Most Left Bank bars have a squat toilet à la Turque, which is to say, a hole in the tile floor of what feels like an extra-large broom closet. It's a water closet – and known in France as WC or le water closet, I think originally, and abbreviated to le water (wat-air).

The hole you piss into is in the center of a raised porcelain basin with two cleated cement footpads on either side of a porcelain hole. After you've used it once you quickly learn what might well have been the origin of the fox trot. When you're done, you gently yank the chain of an overhead box that sends down a cascade of water while you rush out slamming the door behind you before the flood overflows your shoes.

Then there's pissing against buildings, a time-honored practice in France. I don't know if it is an unlawful act but if it is, it's the most frequently broken law in France. A blunt prohibition "Défense de Pisser" is stencilled in black enamel paint on otherwise blank walls of selected buildings, no doubt marking past favorite spots. Repeated smelly sprinklings make clear that even posted walls are not safe.

Government edifices like the Chambre des Députés dignify the matter with the more refined "Défense d'Uriner", though on evidence that does not cut down on offerings. In the case of the Assemblée it is possible that political opinions are being expressed. Possibly for this reason, the government long ago set up outdoor urinals called vespasiennes, named for the Roman emperor Vespasian. In an outburst of altruism Vespasian provided street urinals for the male citizens of Rome and then thoughtfully charged a user's tax each time anyone took a leak. Given a healthy functioning of the urinary tract and bladder, it was an inexhaustible financial resource covering much of the city's budgetary needs.

But in Paris, even without the tax threat, the introduction

of urinoirs did not alter men's old ways of peeing wherever they happened to be as long as they didn't publicly flash their dong.

Never having seen anyone stopped from publicly urinating I have started doing what the pre-Vespasian Romans used to do and on peaceful sunny days enjoy a pleasant outdoor peepee. The other day a woman walking her dog caught me in flagrante delicto against a building and showed much French tact and savoir faire by amiably strolling past in an understanding of the capacity of the human bladder and a certain reality principle. Without breaking stride or commenting she stepped skillfully over the streamlet that dustily meandered from building to street while fighting her dog who, under the sway of a different reality principle, kept tugging her back to the interesting piddle.

Meanwhile bad news. Cleo has received a summons to appear in court. Something to do with her visa? Neither of us understands. She asks if I would mind going with her as her interpreter. At the appointed hour we face a tribunal with the air of posing for a Daumier etching: three judges sitting high up. Quite unreal. I try to listen to their whispered consultations to understand what crime Cleo was being charged with and one of the judges addressing her says she should pay a thousand francs fine and the other two quickly whisper no-no-no back and forth, saying the fine should be more like a hundred francs. "She's a student – a guest in France." "Yes but she's américaine." Buzz buzz, more deliberations, heads put together, and then the judgment: "Whereas in view of blah-blah, not to mention paragraph eight subsection two and furthermore and so forth, a fine: three hundred francs. You are very fortunate, mademoiselle."

Cleo whispers to me: "Should I fight it?"

That scares me more than the judges do. "That's a fifteen-cent fine? Are you insane?"

"But it'll be on my record. What's my crime?"

"I have no idea."

"I'm a student at Smith. Maybe I should get in touch with the school's – "

"Jesus, Cleo, just pay and let's get the hell out of here! They're starting to look irritated."

"But I didn't do anything."

"I think that's the problem. There's maybe something you should have done."

"Like what?"

"I don't know. Visa problem – something – resident card."

Some of the legal French had been over my head.

"Here." I handed her fine to a clerk, a heavily-rouged middle-aged woman, and as we left said a loud thank you over my shoulder to the three Daumier judges while yanking Cleo out of the courtroom, she protesting in loud whispers as we went and me smiling back at the judges in reassurance that she meant no harm.

We head up to the Dôme and I calm her down. I tell her about my visit to Picasso and that comes as another shock. Cleo incredulous that I had called on – oh my God! – the great Pablo Picasso.

"You actually went to see him?" (Amazement at the thought that I would even attempt such a thing.)

"Not exactly. He wasn't there."

"You know where he lives?" (Amazed still, wide-eyed.)

"It's just a few streets from here. But he's never there. He's down south most of the time."

"You went to his studio?" (The amazement continues but slowly yields to helpless admiration.)

I explained that I went up the back stairs to his atelier, up on the top floor. There behind a high iron grill on the open back porch I could see a large barrel brimming with torn-up bits of handsome drawing paper with small traces of ink on them. It was just out of reach.

"What did you do?"

"The concierge five stories down – she yelled up at me to go away."

"Did you explain to her?"

"To a concierge? You don't explain things to a concierge. You would wind up explaining things to the police."

Quite a day. At an outside table at the Dôme a waiter takes our order. Cleo comments on two Frenchmen at a nearby table.

"What are you staring at?" I ask her. It's a day full of wonders.

She has a strange look, a gaze so steady I can't imagine what she's seeing.

"Those two guys. At that table. They're French and belong here. They're at home – it's their café, their boulevard. You know? This is France and they're French. When they make eyes at women they're making eyes at their women. They're in their café, their boulevard. They're not aware how good their lives are. They belong here and don't even know that they belong. They just belong."

I put this down just as she said it, thinking I understand it.

Seeing Yette at her post on the terrasse of the Dôme she asked me the same question about having or rather not having a girlfriend and then asked that her prying be excused. She always saw me alone, and that had made her curious.

I ask if my joining her gives people the impression that she's busy with a client? Not at all. I think she's always glad to have someone to talk with and I'm willing to oblige for my own purposes of learning French. Despite language difficulties I try discussing with her comparative mores, the differences between Jersey City and Paris.

I am embarrassed, of course, to be experiencing so unaccustomed a cultural dislocation and embarrassed also to be telling all this to Yette. I tried explaining that where I had come from, you treated women with respect and respect meant only one thing: keep your hands off. Respect meant No Sex. When you met someone you liked you did not go to bed with her. A different set of rules seemed to apply here and I told Yette I sometimes had difficulty adopting the new rules.

She looked at me, carefully taking it all in, then shaking her head – sadly she delivered a gentle dressing-down, this time on the error of my ways. The problem was in understanding what "respect" meant. Where there was any mutual attraction at all, she pointed out, to give a woman a polite goodnight kiss at the door and walk away and leave her standing there was not respect. It was the male equivalent of a prick tease. It was tantamount to a mild form of cruelty. This seemed to be a theme of hers. Anyone who didn't see that was mentally retarded.

I was being called a retard for a second time. But it made me happy to hear her say that in her view everything I do when I'm with a new woman acquaintance should be calculated to steering her to the nearest bed.

"With a woman, you storm the gates. That's rule number one. But – but – extremely important, even though you're chasing her, you let her come to you, because without her consent you won't get anywhere. It's really a two-step thing. You storm the gates, step one. Step two, she starts to want you. Understand?"

I murmured in English, "Faint heart never won fair lady."

She looked at me suspiciously. "What?"

But, she went on, ignoring any answer I might make, I should never make the mistake of seeing Frenchwomen in the usual tawdry view of them as cliché sexpots who never say no. Frenchwomen enjoy being pursued but they evaluate a man's determination and his desire for them by the ardor of his courtship. They give men credit for enjoying taking the lead and being a little inventive. They're hard-wired that way. Surely I could understand that. Women want men to work for it to show their appreciation. But they reward the effort. Especially because they're after the same thing but aren't going to let on they are. They want the trimmings first.

I'm summing it up here but that was the essence of her lecture. She called me her poor little cabbage and thought it was peculiar that at my age I had such little understanding of these things. Obviously I was some kind of idiot. But then, she had to remind herself, she was dealing with someone from the cultural sticks, the sticks comprising, if I understood her correctly, the continent of North America. To come from such a background was a handicap that was no one's fault. It was just one of those things. Still, one learned.

"Over here it's not unusual for a man and a woman feeling mutual desire to stop whatever they're doing and head for a couch. Or do it standing up, if necessary. On the contrary, mon Dieu, people would think it abnormal if that did not happen."

She was a great teacher and I loved what she was teaching me. To understand women I had to know that they liked men who have a "mélange de douceur et force". And if you had this blend of tenderness and strength you didn't need anything else. Her advice: when a new friend, a woman you've just met at a café, answers that she doesn't mind if you walk her back to her place, you invite yourself up to her room for a drink. The worst she could say is no. If she says OK, come on up, then while she's getting out the brandy glasses or preparing coffee, you go over and put your arms around her in a comforting way. Is there anything wrong in that? Tell her you've been admiring her all evening and hug her around the waist and kiss her. Being hugged feels nice to a woman. Then, not necessarily, but she just might, depending on her mood, pull back the bedcovers so you can continue talking there."

"Just like that?"

"That was what was on your mind, non? And, take my word for it, it was on hers too, or believe me, you wouldn't be up in her room having coffee at eleven o'clock at night in the first place. She was feeling le désir and probably dying to have you the moment she laid eyes on you in the café and knew she had to have you. One way or another you were both heading that way, so, merde, why waste time talking about sonnets? – except maybe to get her a little more in the mood. Women love to be wooed. You'd be surprised at how often a woman wants to make love with a man and is only waiting for him to make the right moves, even though she's been telegraphing him all evening. You know, it's an old joke that the only reason women get dressed is so men will undress them. Women say no to play it safe and appear demure but having their resistance worn down is part of the pleasure. It thrills them that you want them enough to enjoy the pursuit. Men really can be dumb, you know. You, well, you're not dumb, you're just naive. Americans are very sweet people but they're really des petits enfants, you know?"

"The men or the women?"

"Both. But especially the men. It's all very touchant, in a way. You know, touching."

Her advice was that I shouldn't be timid. If I see a woman I like, just go up to her and say hello and see what happens. I might be surprised at how welcome that direct approach might be.

I told her I had tried it once. "I went up to this woman and said 'Bonjour!'"

"So what happened?"

"She stared at me as though I were a maniac. And walked off."

Yette's response was: "She's to be pitied."

I was willing to believe her, even though I was not sure I had the requisite degree of bravery to just walk up and, as she puts it, storm a woman's gates. But then maybe I had been getting it all wrong in the past. I reasoned to myself that as a woman Yette understood women in ways I couldn't imagine and I tried to learn from her as much as I could. Not just about sex but about feelings of friendship and about men and women growing fond of each other and feeling close and falling in love.

"What do you know about love?" Yette asked.

"You keep asking me that."

There was obvious skeptical challenge in the question and I said as much, but she said I needn't worry.

"Nature is on everybody's side. You'll see."

I said that one of the things it was pleasant to be learning was that women had sex on their minds almost as much as men did.

"No," Yette said. "More."

Big change. Cleo has moved in to the Hotel Descartes. She's now installed and happy to have a place of her own – "except for the godawful wallpaper." French wallpaper is a medley of thousands of miniature rose bouquets on a white background. She has covered over this "wall art" with large sheets of white drawing paper except for a small patch, where the bidet is attached to the wall, revealing a sliver of the old wall covering.

I learn all this when she invites me up for coffee to show it off. A large double bed practically fills the room. Its thick lemon-yellow comforter gives the bed a cozy feeling. Over the headboard a framed reproduction shows a Toulouse-Lautrec brothel scene and just below it a brief wall bookshelf with a line-up of Steppenwolf, Tropic of Cancer, Voyage au Bout de la Nuit, Psychopathia Sexualis, Tertium Organum by

somebody named Ouspensky and the collected works of
Kafka. Serving as bookends: two dark-green pinch bottles of
Rémy Martin, one empty, one nearly empty but still working.

She looks lovely sitting in bed propped up by outsized
pillows. I feel privileged being allowed to see her so
informally, in long-sleeved white-flannel nightgown with a
small scarlet-threaded abstract design intricately stitched just
below her throat. Until this moment I have seen her only
dressed, ponytail swinging, and now her dark chestnut hair -
spills from shoulders to pillow to give the tableau a luxurious
feel. Sensing her body warmth under the white sheets and the
Matisse-yellow comforter, my impulse is to crawl in with her
and hug her.

Ah love. Or anyway, ah sex.

And then I catch on. We're approaching the big event –
today's the day: I poured myself a glass of some interesting
red wine she has – a little rusty-tasting.

"You go to Smith to get the right contacts to marry well.
Isn't that what the Seven Sisters are all about?"

"Oh really?" she said. "Is that what a college education is
all about? And who told you I was looking to get married, for
shit sake?"

I almost spilled the wine. "For shit sake?"

"I'll have to be careful when I go back home but I pick
things up from you."

"You're bound to meet someone who's right for you. They
say that's when real magic happens."

"Who said I'm looking?"

"If you were to look."

"I would want someone with a sense of humor. Someone of intelligence. Oh."

"What?"

"You're putting all this down for your memoirs, aren't you?"

I laugh.

"I don't think people write their memoirs in their twenties."

"Well whatever it is you're writing. You keep scribbling things. I saw your sketchpad."

"Just things to remember later. Sort of kind of a diary in a way."

"'My Paris Diary.' Oh wow," she said.

"Don't let's fight."

"I'm just kidding. I hate fighting. I once watched two starfish fighting. They were out to kill each other. It was one of those nature films and it wasn't something you'd enjoy seeing."

Was she serious?

"Starfish fight?"

"Ferociously. They murder each other. Must be some territorial thing."

I had brought a bottle of Vittel as a housewarming gift along with a small bouquet of some tiny flowers whose name I didn't know, a large bar of Swiss chocolate, three Valencia oranges and a package of spaghetti. I sliced the oranges in half and juiced them into a coffee mug while explaining the health benefits of palpating a patient's chest in cases of this kind.

"Don't bother –" she said.

"Oh it's no bother at all."

"– to try to make out. My chest is fine."

"I'll just get in bed and we'll be all cozy." I was enjoying this.

"Don't conclude anything, especially that I'm some kind of tease, because I'm not a tease. But I've never done it before. I should have said something earlier."

"Let's eat first and then talk. You need your strength back."

"This is some seduction scene."

"I'm not seducing you," I lied.

"You're right about that."

She told me where her primus stove was and I assembled my special all-purpose one-size-fits-all pasta dish, Spaghetti Bohème: butter, parsley, basil, garlic. A lot of garlic. She had butter and little jars of different herbs. Surprisingly she even had garlic.

"Garlic smells so good," she said. "I love Italian cooking."

"See? You're feeling better already."

"Okay but do me a favor. Try not to keep climbing into bed with me."

"After we eat, then."

"Even after we eat. Rushing things never works."

"There's something almost perverse about you."

"What perverse? I'm a virgin."

"You're – you're a virgin? At nineteen?" It really surprised me.

"Nineteen's not that old."

I was thinking what reply to make.

"Does that put you off?" she asked.

"I've never talked so openly about these things."

"Oh don't be a twit. I'm the virgin here."

"'Thou still unravished bride of loveliness,'" I said.

"I don't know about the loveliness part but 'thou still' not much longer."

It had all been mapped out apparently and today was the day. First some wine. To take the edge off. With a bottle of red and a bottle of white plus a backup of some brut. Important ingredients for the occasion of losing one's virginity. The wines were to supplement what remained of her Rémy Martin, brought down now from the bookshelf, self-consciously explaining as she did so that she kept the hard stuff for emergencies. I believe she thought she looked sophisticated casually wagging the bottle by its neck as she brought it over. There was so little cognac left I wondered what the recent emergencies had been.

All businesslike now: "What happens first?" she asked.

A performance was being staged: first I do this and then you do that.

"Customarily one strips," I said. "Not altogether necessary or obligatory but it adds to the –."

"Please don't make jokes."

She poured herself most of what was left of the Rémy Martin and with a violent grimace shuddered it down. Hearing me uncork the champagne with a pop she snatched the bottle from my hand by its crinkly gold-foiled neck and tilted it up to swig from it directly and realized too late the magnitude of her mistake as wine in a violent flood effervesced over her face, throat, chest, bubbling to the floor. Watching her wipe her sopping cheeks and chin with the back of her hand and then with a towel grabbed from my hand, I suggested she not anaesthetize herself but slow down and relax and enjoy things. She thought that an excellent suggestion and took another long slug of cognac before I could stop her. It was the last of the Remy Martin, and I could almost begin to feel her hangover the next day.

Turning shyly away, she undid a man's button-down Oxford shirt, a faint orange job probably bought from ye olde campus shoppe called The Young Miss. She tossed the shirt to a chair and snaked her Black Watch wool skirt down her hips and stepped free of it as I got naked and slipping between the sheets watched the ever-pleasant sight of a woman undressing. Reaching behind her back to unhook a new-looking black-lace bra, she hunched her shoulders abruptly forward to induce the bra straps to slide down her arms and free her breasts. Her tan nipples were barely darker than the surrounding skin and as modest as Olympia's in Manet's painting. Next she slipped her sheer nylon stockings off and removed the English garter belt (her "suspenders") bought in London.

"Et – voici les buttocks."

And of course they were two perfectly lovely nineteen-year-old buns that many women would kill to have. She skivvied out of chic black panties ("knickers") with their black lace trim, revealing a tantalizing glimpse of matted brown fur before she slid under the covers and smoothly, swiftly, pulled the sheet up to her chin and snuggled alongside me and closed her eyes. In drunken self-comfort she innocently slid an arm round my neck to rest her cheek against my shoulder, apparently enjoying the unfolding events as something happening in some hazy interior world. As we clasped each other in physical contentment she turned a half-lidded gaze toward me.

"You think maybe another drink before we –?"

"I don't recommend it."

"Whoa – the room."

Abruptly she sat up to make the walls and floor stop sailing off.

"Your body. I've never seen a man's . . . you know, his . . .I mean without . . ."

I turned her face to mine and with a kind of desperation she impulsively kissed me with champagne lips. And when I touched her breasts and felt the hardening of her small pebbled nipples, shyness made her press herself self-protectively against my chest to stop me from further inspection. Inhaling her youthful fragrance, I could feel her breathing change as she shut her eyes in trust now of whatever was going to happen next.

Later, as we lay side by side, she said if making love was anything like what she had just experienced she was surprised at the fuss made over it. I explained that not being an earth-shattering experience the first time was practically the norm but I don't think I convinced her. And anyway the question became irrelevant when she froze, hurled herself out from under the covers, hand clamped on mouth, and dashed across the room to vomit into the sink.

"God!"

Coming back wiping her face on a towel she said, "You poisoned me!" She was flipped-out irrational. "Some friend, you are! You're trying to poison me."

"It's OK," I reassured her, "you're just deep-crocked, that's all."

Absurdly, after what she had just said, she crept back into bed and put an arm around my neck and nuzzled my throat. I held her close until she grew still and from where her head lay on my chest, I heard dozing sounds and, mixed in with the lovely scent of her body, got a whiff of sour breath.

Next Day. Things better this morning though she has taken the event as a personal failure, or, feeling no pleasure, concludes she suffers from a physiological defect. We made love twice that morning and tried several more times in the afternoon but no use. We were just going through the motions. Lying together and hugging seemed to console her. She complained only that she could easily do without a certain crotchy discomfort when she peed and made a terrible pun about having been deflowered du mal.

"I guess I'm not much of a piece of ass," she said, genuinely shocking me

"Is that how they talk in Northampton?"

She's convinced she's a freak of nature, one of those frigid women Krafft-Ebing did psychiatric studies about. She's now studying his book of case histories, installing herself in bed for a long read.

I assure her she's no freak. But privately I wonder if she might not be right. I've heard that certain women are born frigid, just the opposite of some who were such nymphomaniacs you could kill yourself trying to satisfy them. When you meet a new woman, how can you be sure you're getting a fully-functioning batteries-included human female? Trial and error is the only way to proceed, I suppose, if you don't want to get locked in for life with a huge mistake you once made in your long-ago youth and spend the rest of your life regretting.

But being involved with her I feel responsible and determined to proceed with patience. It's the moral obligation of the experienced person to help a novice through the important life passage of making love for the first time. I wouldn't want her to remain disappointed with sex and have the disillusionment ruin whatever romantic fantasies she might be enjoying – a beautiful love affair in Paris, a Left Bank romance, first man-woman relation, all of the above and more.

Not feeling much of anything, she chats as we make love,

me on autopilot, her voice in my face as I labor over her –
which is how it feels, like work – while harboring visions of
ending the friendship and telling her it has all been a sad
mistake and offering her my sincere apologies. We would part
on good terms and remain friends and nobody would be hurt.
Some general idea like that.

What's stopping me is that I can't leave her while she's
convinced she's some terrible biological phenomenon called a
frigid woman. I have to persist making love all the while
listening to her passively accepting the effort as she reports
odd bits of information from wherever her mind wanders – the
death toll of a recent flood in the Punjab, some thoughts on
symmetry in Cézanne's composition, a reminder to buy some
good olive oil for salad. She behaves like a patient and
accommodating friend stretched out uncomplainingly under
me and waiting for me to finish whatever it is I have to be
doing with her body before I let her retake full possession of
it.

I try acting the kindly old sex counselor, the Pro from
North Jersey, sharing with her what I had picked up from a
much older brother's ancient marriage manual from the 1920s.
The book's dust jacket had a photo of the author, a Belgian or
Dutch sex expert, with a sharply-trimmed beard making him
resemble the playing-cards king of spades. He devoted much
space to what he described as our need to understand the
importance of the clitoris in today's woman. If I didn't know
more than the usual superficial amount about Cleo's clitoris it
was because at the age when I first read about the needs of the
contemporary woman and the location and importance of
today's clitoris, I was still living with the hope of seeing a real
flesh-and-blood clit, not the pallid pink pimple shown in the
book's two-tone illustrations. The marital guide made female
genitals sexless. The vulva and the thigh framing it in the
schematic diagram looked like a knothole in a plank of wood.
Now that I had seen one, a real one – after an afternoon of
happy wine guzzling, Cleo's bashfully allowing me a chummy
and much-appreciated closeup – I find it difficult to believe
that that small pip of a thing performs wonders it's given
credit for.

In its more explicit sections the book had an annoying way of switching to words of Latin derivation when it discussed the clitoris as the erectile organ of the vulva. But then after reemphasizing the importance of the efficient functioning of a woman's erectile organ in today's world, the text undermined its own message by asserting that the ideal of human sexual intercourse was mutual simultaneous orgasm in penetrative sex, which, okay, some people could argue is true, but the author went so far as to assert was the only valid sex act.

But it was a waste of time going into all this with Cleo, who strangely wasn't interested in her organ and its erectility, or at least not in any public discussion of it and rightly thought its efficient functioning was nobody's goddam business. What interested her more was knowing about the lovers I'd had and why men saw Frenchwomen as something extraordinary, or whatever it was men saw them as.

I said my opinion was that it isn't Frenchwomen who are extraordinary but visitors to Paris emerging from the hinterlands, which was to say, from almost any other country of the world – they are the extraordinary ones. They just can't get over the mores of the French or their openness in talking about sex in an unembarrassed way, and unembarrassedly doing things that others either didn't do or didn't admit publicly to doing, and certainly didn't discuss. In fact, I said, Frenchwomen actually have shortcomings, which is something you never hear any talk about, and that they can even get a little boring on the subject of sex.

"Boring?"

I tried to explain that companionship in a foreign language is like caressing a woman with your gloves on. After French girls make love they become boudoir philosophers – which though interesting-sounding in a book is a bore in the bedroom. They meditate out loud. "What is love really? Do I love this person genuinely? Or do I love him because he loves me? And in the end, if it's the latter, isn't that just a form of self-love?" With a theme like that, Annette or Paulette can go on for several minutes until you begin to think you've crawled into bed with a logician.

Cleo wanted to know if I believed in love. Of course, I said, who doesn't? But I didn't get sex mixed up with love.

"Why not?"

She laughed, a real amused laugh.

"Why not?" she wanted to know. "Sex and love go together, no?"

She launched into a minilecture, showing an understanding of things that surprised me coming from a nineteen-year-old. I forget her exact words but what it amounted to was that a cock may be a lovely thing to have, but a cock without love to go with it would not get very far in life. She said there were moments when she wondered if men really did have feelings, and when I asked her how come she knew so much about things, she said – pleased with herself in a teenage way – "Oh I've been around." Her freshness and naïveté suddenly made me feel it would be easy to fall in love with her. I have to smile now as I look back at what I had once hoped or wished to find in Paris and remembered Stendhal and his seduction of women and thought now that seduction combined with love is better than anything he had had.

To reduce or eliminate any worries Cleo might have, I compressed Yette's seminar on contraception: "Bidet 101". I told her about the fancy plumbing fixtures of three-or-more-star hotels that have a geyser shooting straight up the middle with strategic intent, where in ordinary bidets women had to do some scooping up by hand. The trick, of course, was not to wait after making love but use the bidet immediately and let the pull of gravity, the temperature of the water and manual persuasion do the work. Women who hopped out of bed to do that so soon after making love assured me it did not spoil their pleasure. On the contrary, getting the washing quickly out of the way actually improved the sexual experience by removing any fear of pregnancy that would otherwise spoil the long post-orgasmic pleasure.

Cleo listened with interest as I, self-appointed lecturer on sex, called attention to the fact that there were doctors back home who warned that soap desensitized the vagina. My thought was to make her aware of differing opinions and thus have true choice. These doctors contended too that the bidet was not a reliable method of contraception.

"Is that true?"

There was no need to worry. The French liked to make love, not babies, and had complete confidence in the bidet. And the continuing low population of France, a country where condoms were not highly thought of, spoke for itself. In fact France's stagnant rate of population growth was of such long standing that the Assemblée Nationale paid parents a pension for a certain number of children born, and any family producing twelve babies were received as honored guests at the Elysée Palace, where the patriotic mama and papa were bussed on both cheeks by the President of the Republic and handed a check for a million francs.

"No, I mean is it true that soap desensitizes the vagina?"

"Oh," I said. "No. You don't need much soap inside. It's mostly the water and temperature that do the trick."

I assured her that Parisians had no such fears, and besides, the few girlfriends I'd had had never complained, and I'd learned to trust the method. Besides, American doctors would have trouble convincing me that at this moment a couple of million Frenchwomen were walking around the streets of Paris with desensitized vaginas.

Week Later. Cleo, becoming more and more depressed about not having an orgasm, decided – with my encouragement – that the best thing to do was to put the whole idea of orgasms out of her mind and do whatever we were in the mood to do. And that is what we did.

And of course that was when it happened.

One afternoon, having set off on one of her transcoital travelogues, Cleo was complaining about not understanding an Eisenstein film we had seen at the local cinema. It was a film of outtakes experimenting with sound: a soprano singing while the screen surreally showed surf crashing on a beach. She said, "I found it bewil –" and her voice cracked weirdly and her breathing went horribly spastic and stopped – choked off, it sounded like. I thought she was having a heart attack. Shocked into a mid-thrust halt I wondered what could have gone wrong. But then seeing her face contorting into a silent scream, it all at once became clear what she was suddenly experiencing, and seeing it my own pleasure erupted in reflex to her up-thrusting hips urging me not to stop but go on – go on – go – uuuhhh! It took some moments for her ragged breathing and intense gasps on the inhales to quiet down before she could tell me that there had been a quivery throbbing and that must have been the – she looked for words to describe the astonishingly beautiful – the marvellously astonishingly beautiful thing that had just happened. In fact was still happening – and was visible in the red warmth and all-over glow on her face as she placed her head lovingly against my chest.

"Oh my!"

Nature had certainly given Cleo a wonderful supply of hormones. Because it was now pure Chaucer and Boccaccio – the tale of the newly-awakened virgin and the locust-eating hollow-cheeked ascetic. After each obedient and uncomplaining trip to the bidet, Cleo wobbled back to bed for more. It's possible she was trying to make up for earlier frustrations, but for whatever reason, it became twice, three times a day, four times a day, even a sleepy fifth once, waking in the middle of the night before slumping together in sapped exhilaration.

Some of the time we didn't take our clothes off but went at it bundled in layers of pullover, skirt, slip, pants and two sets of underwear while maintaining rhythm without falling out. We became quite adept.

Cleo dubbed me "The Plunger" and she was "Doll Tearsheet" – trying shyly to please ("What's a blow job – I mean, I know what it is but how do you – I mean, what exactly is it?"), on warmer days acting the wily seductress wearing the latest and briefest in French lingerie as an incitement to feats of endurance. Yesterday she formulated a plan for keeping me in permanent top form. I had told her that during the war Parisian women sometimes shared their week's meat ration with their partner to add to his virility and their mutual happiness. Cleo went shopping and came back with two biftecks to sizzle on her small Sterno cooker, and after nibbling at hers while watching me steadily working away at mine, she delicately manoeuvred her uneaten portion toward me with what I believe she thought was her Giaconda smile.

There has certainly not been post coitum omne animal triste. The thought made us laugh as Cleo waited for the famous postorgasmic sadness to hit. And it didn't. The more we made love, the happier we felt. And the happier we felt, the more we enjoyed working afternoons at the Colarossi studio in a prolonged afterglow of the morning and mid-morning boffs, after which, at the post-work end of the day and followed by a virility-fueling meal at Mme Novak's, we headed back to bed for more post coitum animal happy as hell.

We had discovered that Cleo's room is directly below Yette's and sometimes in the night, with only the light from the Rue Delambre dimly illuminating the room, we make a pot of coffee and like conspirators listen to the stirrings above. I had introduced Yette and Cleo at the Dôme one day and she and I now listened to Yette entertaining a client and tried imagining how they were able to do it given her Mt. Everest of a body. Does he climb up on top and lie beached at the summit, but if he does that, how then does he manage to get it in? We think this out of affection for Yette but partly also out of anatomical interest – and a liking for the youthful spirit that lies buried in that mass of flesh. On one occasion she and her client went at it twice, Cleo punning, "Yette again," covering her mouth to smother a laugh while listening to the bed rhythmically bumping Yette's floor and our ceiling in a soft thump thump thump thump of human copulation speeding up to a faster thump thump thump of the home stretch and then distant moans of ultimate fulfillment, the performance then abruptly terminating in an unreal silence. Then plumbing sounds and the quiet swish-gurgle of old hotel pipes and distant middle-of-the-night water-splashings. Followed by more silence and then the soft discreet thud of cushioned footsteps on the hallway's thickly carpeted stairs of someone descending to the foyer.

The latest. Naturally curious to know more about men and what their bodies are like, Cleo arranges me in bed and makes pen-and-inks of the genitals and starts an oil. She likes their colour ("dusky pastel café au lait with a plum blush") and while working reaches over for a rearranging touch, smiling at the genitals shifting with a will of their own. ("Did I make that happen?" – the smile holding a whole adolescence of happiness.) She wants to paint it and would call the painting "Not-So-Still Life". She declares that if she had equipment like that dangling between her legs she would keep it standing all day. Meanwhile seeing her half-reclining, legs doubled sideways, I enjoy seeing the furrow of her soft-haired cunt in a crease of thighs, an unguarded view of a lovely young woman's privates.

With the experiences I've had I'm aware now that I've never lived in intimacy with a woman. So much of sharing quarters comes as a surprise. I've known women so briefly that I've never been privy to the everyday trivia of living with a woman, like bending over the sink to brush my teeth in the morning and finding a delicacy of panties sudsily soaking. And intimacies like catching sight of a furtive feminine hand dislodging wedged panties from butt crack, squaring that with a male view of femininity – the panties of course wedging up tight again as panties seem destined to do. Or to see Cleo laughing so hard at a joke that she frantically makes a classic gesture most men live and die without ever seeing – snug-jamming her palm against crotch in an anxiously puffing race to the toilet.

It has become a winter of quickies on a bed sheet terminally rumpled like a study in folds by Dürer's worst pupil on drugs. The effect is enhanced by our habit of using the bed as a picnic ground for our midnight mainstay of spaghetti in a varying menu of accompanying sauces (Cleo's Spaghetti Essex: Brussel sprouts and anchovies), plus baguettes and ficelles, rounds of camembert, bean soups of varying impromptu components and a tossed green salad always. Between meals, the bed makes a cozy place for listening to the BBC Third Programme and Radio Luxembourg while sipping, depending on mood and weather, coffee, a warming Bovril, or a good cheap red from the wine shop below, heated and served with a big cinnamon stick standing up in it. We have instructed the sleepy-eyed Toulousaine who dusts the room and makes the bed to skip us except once a week to change the sheets. Dust and personal disorder are preferable to a knock on the door as we're slipping it in, going at it full-steam or breathlessly recovering.

Cleo wants to know if all the things Henry Miller has written about Paris are true and I tell her that as far as I know they pretty much are. But his jabberwocky and showoffy words are of a kind found only in books, like chthonian, and should be ignored. They're just showoffy words and never used except by someone with no formal education pretending he has one.

"For example," I ask her, "what does 'fuliginous' mean?"

"Fuck if I know." (She has been picking things up from me.)

She wants to know if I've had adventures of the kind Miller describes. I have not. She doesn't believe me and reminds me of wild moments I've told her about. Like which? Well, like the party we went to in the sculptor's studio just under Chez Novak's kitchen window, where Winnie, a plump African-American painter's model from New York, took her clothes off, facing each of us seated on cushions on the plaster-dust floor and with her crotch at mouth level tried to entice someone to "touftouf" her, complaining that her fires were burning her up. There were no takers for touftoufing Winnie and putting her fires out, but, just mildly drunk enough not to be unhappy about it, she sprawled her bronze body behind us on the filthy white-dusted floor, and when I looked again, she and a sculptor just down from Liverpool and getting his first eyeful of la vie bohème were silently humping in a corner, Winnie smashed enough to think they were invisible, and he shy and still wearing his overcoat, and Cleo, not wanting to be rude by staring openly taking it all in with furtive glances and gleaming eyes and happy sideward looks at me. Like that wild moment.

More quiet afternoons in Montparnasse. Cleo saying she'd give anything to know all the things that go on in my head and me laughing: "Actually, I'd like to know too."

The window is open wide. It's a nice day outside. She's postorgasmic cheerful. Life is wonderful.

"Without love it's all just fucking, don't you think?"

"I dunno. What's wrong with just fucking?"

"Would you be happy with that? – I mean if it was just that?"

"I don't think I would be unhappy."

"Yes, but would you be happy?" Suddenly impatient at the slowness of my response: "Well I hope not all men are as indecisive about it as you are. There is such a thing as love, don't you think? Or do you think life is all pussy, as you put it?"

I know my lines. "Yes," I say, "absolutely, sex combined with love is the best."

"Wow, does that ever sound sincere!"

"Hey, give I a break."

"I would like to think that men care about more than just pussy."

"That's not a very intelligent way to talk about men, as if men were all the same. And besides, I can tell you life is more than just pussy."

"Sorry, I forgot. There's also cleavage."

But she's in a happy mood and there's no jarring her out of it. She goes on out of simple curiosity: "Does Jay have a girlfriend?"

"Loads of them. Serially."

"That's like having none."

"He said he used to have one special one in New Orleans. That's where he's from, New Orleans. N'Awlins."

"What happened?"

"As he explains it, she was studying to become a psychologist but felt drawn to self-degradation, so right away there was a conflict there."

"So it's over, then?"

"I think definitely. He said she had a fine brain and nice tits and said such combinations are rare."

Cleo laughed briefly. "Men."

"He said he was impressed by hers."

"Her what? Her brains?"

"No, the combination. He said one without the other would never be the same. He's quite a connoisseur."

"Of tits, you mean."

"Well, you know . . ."

"Yeah. Men."

Overheard at the Dôme:

"Are you a writer?"

"I don't drink that much."

I know very little about the art world and Jay fills me in. It began when I asked him if he was going to have a show. Jay explains that having a show of your work makes sense only if a gallery invites you to show. Otherwise all that happens is you pay the rent of the gallery and they hang your paintings.

"How do you get a review?"

"You invite the critic of a paper to your show. He comes in and heads for the display case of art books, and extracts a handsome and very expensive art book and walks out. He takes his fee in advance."

"For his review."

"Exactly. The gallery dealer of course puts the art book on your bill."

"What bill?"

"The month's rent to have your show. The critic puts a two-sentence notice in his newspaper column saying the public could expect to be hearing your name in the future – and there's your review. You then show this review around New York and brag how you had a one-man show in Paris. The only problem is that the dealers in New York know all about these things and know they're worthless."

We decide that for the most part the whole art scene is dishonest. But even apart from that, we agree that painters would have to be naïve to expect to make money from art.

At the Dôme. Jay: "What I like about the French is that sex is out in the open." He's on his favorite topic. "And at the same time they're very discreet about the subject."

We talked about "back home" and the transatlantic liners ferrying tourists to Paris, only some of them coming to see the art treasures of the Louvre and the others for an assortment of reasons but in Jay's view the other reasons all having to do with sex.

"You have a one-track mind," I said.

"It's really a monomania," he agrees completely and then goes right on. Jay is not someone you can offend easily and he was now in one of his talkative moods. He said the pleasures of bed are not openly discussed by tourists but spoken of in a rolling-of-the-eyes oo-la-la way about how Frenchwomen like to zigzig a lot. That and their other interest in life."

"Which is?"

"Blowjobs. The tourists back in the East Armpit, Missouri, say things like, 'Oh the museums!' (the Mona Lisa) 'and the food!' (kwee-ZEEN), but secretly they come to Paris as a voulez-vous-coucher destination and contribute their bit toward making sex France's number-one growth industry. I read that in the Wall Street Journal."

I said, "Glands will be glands, I suppose."

"Glands will be glands."

We were starting to get philosophical, Jay filling me in about good places to meet women for puss-ihhh. The best spots were around the Sore-Bun. The whole Sammy-Shell area was good too, in fact you couldn't go wrong in any of the Bull Meesh cafes. They were packed with female students from Eastern Europe, and as Jay emphasized, each came equipped with a puss-ihhh. It's a monomania, all right. But sometimes I think he's pulling everybody's leg with all that talk. Hard to tell sometimes.

Cleo appears from some shopping she's been doing. What has she bought? Nothing. Just window shopping.

"Hello," I say. "Come and join us"

"Hi," Jay says.

"Hello, everybody" Cleo says.

Cleo has been on one her forays around the Left Bank, getting to know Paris, and reports an American couple she overheard at the Closerie des Lilas.

"This guy says, 'Wow! Right here, right at this table? Hemingway? He sat right here?' and she says, 'Oh Herman, for god sake, don't come all unglued. Who gives a happy shit where Hemingway sat?'"

Jay takes this in but then continues where he left off.

"It's been my experience that women like to fuck just as

much as men do. Maybe more."

I look over at Cleo showing no emotion as she comments: "Is this some discovery of yours?"

"In Montparnasse," Jay goes on, "all you have to do to find a lover is show up. Friends who frequent the same cafés have all pretty much had each other."

"What's it like in Hoboken?"

That's my contribution, an attempt to change the subject.

"Hoboken?" Cleo asks. "What does Hoboken have to do with this?"

"For one thing, Jay was born there."

"I was born in Hoboken but my family moved away when I was a month old."

"Where were you born?" Cleo asks me.

"Me? Jersey City. Contiguous to Hoboken."

"Sorry to hear that."

"What, that they're contiguous?"

"No, that you were born in Jersey City."

"Me too."

"Or Hoboken. Jesus," Cleo said.

"Don't knock it," I say. "Hoboken is life."

Jay asks if I ever made out with Mme. Verger. I glance at Cleo again and again try to change the subject.

Cleo says: "Would you gentlemen prefer it if I left so you could talk?"

Jay glances over at a woman just arriving. She sits down at a table at the far end of the terrasse.

"You look as though you know her?" I comment, following his look.

"Not yet."

She looks in her mid-twenties. Black high heels and a chic pants-suit. The waiter brings her a fine and I wait to see how long it will take Jay to make his move. She resembles someone I saw him with once, a young Greek-French girl whose family thought she was helping send her brother through the St. Cyr military academy. She told Jay her family thought she did fashion modeling in one of the couturier houses, which was why she was always dressed so chicly. But in fact she was doing quite well as a fille operating on the Champs-Elysees.

"Where is she now?"

"Gone."

Some American GI had fallen in love with her and taken her to live on his ranch in Wyoming. Or as she called it VEE-o-mang. Massachusetts was Ma-SA-shoe-tits.

The woman at the other end of the terrace never leaves Jay's radar. As she sips her fine and looks out at the boulevard we try to pin down a quality she has, agreeing it was a pleasing blend of youthfulness and womanly chic.

"Have you ever noticed," I ask, "how on Frenchwomen the muscles on the two sides of the lower lip are prominent? Like two small bumps below the lips."

I theorize that it comes from the pronunciation of the letter u. It's impossible to say a French u without puckering your lower lip, and if you do that a thousand times a day it's bound to affect the development of those muscles.

"Well," Jay says lazily getting up. "That may not be the only way they develop those muscles."

We watch him move into action. He goes over to the woman's table and with a warm Jay smile says something as he casually pulls up a chair beside her. She smiles back. We watch discreetly, then forget them and look at the people passing by and the taxis forming a rank in the middle of the boulevard. When we look back to Jay and the woman they're turning the corner of Delambre.

The waiter comes by and asks was there anything else before going over and cleaning off the woman's table. He goes back inside.

Cleo and I are enjoying a nice peaceful early-afternoon feeling when Jay comes back. He has been gone barely twenty-five minutes and even from far away you can see his contented look.

"She was on her way to join her fiancé," he says to me. "She's supposed to meet him on the Right Bank at three o'clock."

He sits down in the wicker chair and stretches out his legs.

"I like the way they kill time over here," he says. He sounds relaxed.

"Unless, of course, you're the fiancé waiting for her over on the Right Bank."

"Hey," Jay laughs. "What do you think he's doing till three o'clock?"

Later. Cleo wants to know if anything "Krafft-Ebingish" has ever happened to me or my friends and I say no, but then recall the time when Norbert, a handsome French composer my age or a bit older, met two sixteen-year-old girls at Patrick's Café who wanted to share him as their very first lover ever. His place had just room enough for an old upright piano and he made love with one while the other played Débussy and then the girls switched places. Norbert himself told me this.

"I thought those things happened only in books," Cleo said happily.

"In books and in Paris."

Cleo loved hearing about that, but her favorite "Krafft-Ebingish" story was the one about the young model at the Pommier, Angèle, who in a jam-packed Métro became aware that a teenage boy behind her was pressing his front against her bottom in a way no longer justified by the thinning out of the crowd. Remembering her own adolescent ardor, she didn't say anything or even react to the softly rhythmic pounding against her accepting butt. What could the poor kid do? And who was he harming? He was just carried away and it would soon be over. But when she got off at her stop and the boy descended with her and began trailing behind her, she turned and demanded:

"Once wasn't enough?"

Great fun getting to know Cleo and just what Jersey City had needed. Too bad I had never met anyone like her there. Occasionally we dined out, trying places where I had eaten before finding Novak's. The more I saw of her, the less odd her looking in mirrors seemed. But I couldn't deceive myself for long and began to believe I was only imagining improvements. The truth was that her peering into every mirror she passed and making faces at herself made me uncomfortable.

But even with that I felt it hard not to be drawn to her northern European loveliness though doubting I could spend the rest of my days with her. Which made me feel sad. When Cleo asked if thoughts of marriage ever entered my mind, I said that they had been known to enter and swiftly exit. She smiled but said nothing, leaving me hoping she understood it didn't mean I didn't care for her. I did care. But I didn't want to marry someone who spends her life gazing in mirrors.

She had been adopted at birth and maybe there was a strange family history that only the adoption agency knows about. It was entirely possible that her biological mother couldn't go to sleep without wearing tennis shoes to bed.

I asked about her biological family. She said nobody knew anything about them. She wished she knew who her real parents were. She didn't think there was anything in anybody's genetic makeup about looking in mirrors, at least not that she was aware of. I asked if it was a tic and she laughed and said no. It went back to her adolescence, when she saw herself for the first time in a three-way mirror and decided she was ugly.

"I thought it was only your succinct bum you were unhappy about."

"Well, that in particular."

My comment about marriage had an effect, of course, as I should have known it would. Even so it took me by surprise when she told me one day that the time had come for her to be going to Italy. No, the marriage question had nothing to do with it. She had had the plan to go to Rome and Florence long before our first meeting at Chez Novak, in fact back in Northampton. The plan had recently been elaborated to include Giovanna, a classmate at Smith – tall golden-haired Giovanna from Provence, who hated the Northampton boys for the way they had mocked her: Miss Iron Pants from Southern France. Giovanna was bored to death with Smith and dark New England days and the slushy winters of the north. Europe! That was the place to live! By combining resources with Cleo they could do a tour of Italy ending in sunny Venice, where an uncle of hers lived – her favorite uncle.

I tried picturing life without Cleo. But I couldn't see taking her back to my world of puritanical neighbors, not someone, like her, from sophisticated Fairfield County, Connecticut. It was unthinkable. She'd hate it and neither of us would be happy.

We said goodbye, me in a haze of emotions not wanting her to leave but not knowing how to dissuade her without permanently committing myself to her. Cleo said she would miss me.

At the Gare de Lyon as people boarded the train, I put her bags in her compartment and kissed her goodbye with a long hug. There was a shrill peep and I was outside on the platform watching Cleo waving back to me from an open corridor window as I walked beside the slowly moving train, then walking faster to keep up with her, and then seeing her face growing smaller as the train bore her away.

And I wondered if this really was the last time I'd ever see her. It didn't seem possible. But I supposed this was the way it had to be.

Review Northeast (?) has accepted my Yette piece for the Fall Number. Do I accept psychological compensation, no payment? Yes.

Mme Verger: "How good to be seeing you more frequently." She commented I did not act as cheerful as recently. I explained that my petite amie had gone to Italy with a classmate from America to spend a holiday together but it was all for the best.

Mme Verger looked skeptical.

"Where there's genuine love between a man and a woman they don't lose each other so easily. One does not walk away from love if the love is real."

I felt confused. I don't know if I would have fallen in love with Cleo if she had not left. I had not wanted to go with her, yet I felt enormously sad at her absence – her loss. A week went by, then two and postcards began appearing in the letter tray outside the concierge's loge. The first ones ("Having fun – miss you") were postmarked Pompeii and Taormina and were followed by two from Positano. Then a barrage of cards (one starting: "My dear fucker"), all with breathless phrases about "la bell' Italia!!!" I imagined her in Italy and in her exuberant scribbles felt the heat of the Italian sun. She urged me to grab the next train down, adding that Giovanna would like to meet me, and underneath that, in someone else's florid but disciplined scrawl, "Come <u>down</u>!" Which I would have loved to do but how? How could I go? – with what money? Then a folded card showing Michelangelo's "David" with, at the bottom, "For Comparison Purposes!!" addressed to "The Champ!" And within the card's fold, loose curled hairs and the note: "From the people down south, with their fondest memories."

Then after a long silence a card from Firenze described an Italian medical intern she had met – Ezio. Ezio was an opera lover and handsome and very romantic and found her a "'<u>sexy</u> bella ragazza' (!!!) – Moi!" He said he was madly in love with her and hinted at marriage, and Cleo asked what I thought. Replying poste restante American Express, I told her how happy I was she had found someone simpatico and confessed I was jealous. Actually I was more than jealous and suppressed the surprising wrench I felt as I pushed out of my mind the thought that I might have made one of the biggest mistakes of my life.

In cafés and streets I would see someone who looked like Cleo and wondered at the strange possessiveness I felt but had never suspected. I wrote back warning her of fortune hunters and that the genuine article, a man who truly loved her, would always be willing to wait – and secretly hoped Ezio was only out to grab what he could and would be found out.

A new card announced that she and Ezio were coming up to Paris so that she could show him Montparnasse, adding that she felt he and I would like each other. When there was another silence, one lasting several weeks, I interpreted that to mean the real end for Cleo and me. I assumed she and Ezio had moved in together and maybe even were married by now and expecting a bambino. But more time passed and a note arrived one day saying she and Ezio had broken up. Ezio had a roving eye,

She asked if anything would ever work out for her, telling me how terrible she felt. She felt sure her big bum had something to do with it and admitted she did have strange ways of behaving at times and Ezio had not liked it and at least was blunt about it. He honestly cared for her as a person and said he felt molto molto bad, and swore on his grandmother's grave that he had not set out to be a traitor (the words becoming more operatic as he went along – traditore! O Dio!). But after finishing his studies in Florence he would be moving to Palermo, where (un bel di, no doubt) he would be setting up a general practice. But he wanted her to know that she would "sempre, sempre" be his cara and he would never forget her, and after another couple of addios thrown in and a final swear on his grandmother's grave it was over.

Cleo said she felt fortunate in having Giovanna with her for support. Giovanna, for her part, now considered Ezio and his "fucking rampant eyeball" an enormous Tuscan turd, and the same went for Ezio's grandmother and all her fucking cousins too.

In the end Cleo said she missed me but for now would stay on with Giovanna and hoped we'd keep in touch even after I returned to the States. She missed America, something she thought would never happen after Paris, and said to be sure to let her know if I ever went back – stay in touch. And a final, separate paragraph:

"Do you miss me?"

I think if there was a moment in my life when I began to see things in some more serious light – if I ever had the faintest intimation of the beginnings of maturity – it came with Cleo's taking off for Italy and me stupidly letting her go. Of course I missed her. It felt as though I were experiencing myself in life for the first time. Not the letting go part but the regret at having let her go.

After that, everything seemed different. She became a ghost. I saw her everywhere. I fell asleep seeing her beside me and woke up thinking about her and reminding myself that her staring into mirrors didn't matter. I should not have let her go. Had I had made a mistake?

I would be selfish and urge her to come back. But how could I if financially I could not hang on? My GI Bill was ending. I had had only one piece published. And there was another thing. Paris was no longer the Paris I had left New York for. The French had traits and ugly behavior I had not noticed before. There were no longer spacious boulevards but only trafficked avenues in a large city with walls that had "Yankee Go Home" chalked messages and I heard Stendhal's youthful enthusiasm shrivelling into a weariness with Paris: "Was this all there was to Paris? Was this the Paris I had longed for?"

One morning I felt a surprising rage at the once-friendly ticket seller at the St. Germain Métro station who a hundred times before had sold me tickets and now refused entrance because I was a franc short – a third of a penny! Her indignant shriek "Ah non, monsieur!" was a slap, and I had to remind myself not to let small-minded feelings take away the Paris that had been so beautiful merely because I could no longer have it.

I took stock of my life: drafted into the army at eighteen, sent to Europe, at twenty-one back to finish at university and returned to Europe, this time to live in Paris, and now, almost twenty-three, returning to where I had started and trying to make sense of that life.

My time in Paris has been spent close to poverty and now all money was gone. If I go to the Cinémathèque, the Champs-Elysées, Montmartre, I go on foot, replacing the cardboard inside one of my shoes to cover a growing hole. Haircuts are simple. I lop off fringes that stick out and in true artistic feeling have little interest in doing anything more about it than that. I've even skipped a few meals to save money and to see what it would be like to really starve. I found that two days of not eating were difficult to get through but by the third day there was no hunger left, and on day four I woke up elated and fresh, my body feeling cool even though the open window brought in warm springtime air. It was when I felt it would be a fine and beautiful thing to spend the rest of my life on a nice comfortable bed with an afternoon breeze flowing over me that I decided I had better end the experiment, and, lightheaded, remembering the smells of Mme Novak's cassoulets and gigots, eased out of bed and went up to Montparnasse and ordered soup and pâté de campagne and a tournedos, and then a nice ripe runny camembert followed by an endive salad and, topping things off, a rice pudding, and afterwards a leisurely espresso at Patrick's with lots of sugar and a zest of lemon. Except for the coffee, all of the above on credit.

I don't know how the expatriates of the twenties could have gone home once they'd seen Paree and wonder how they adapted to repatriation and what work they'd found in Trenton or Sioux City – because there was now, if I went back, or when I went back, the thought of earning a living at something I would probably not like.

In all the months in Paris I had dreamed of learning many things about life. Now, no longer dreams, they were a part of me, and Cleo too was a part of me, an unanticipated good part. I had not expected anyone like her to appear in my life – that I would have the good fortune to know someone like her. And I wished her well.

I went to say goodbye to Yette. Not to disturb her, I waited till noon, and when I tapped on her door a groggy "Oui?" came back. Stepping into a darkly-curtained room I could make her out, propping herself up on an arm, and as I marveled at her figure, the elbow as big around as a normal woman's thigh, she turned her face toward me, eyes blinking against the hall light streaking across her blanket. She smiled as she made out who it was and waved away my apology for rousing her from sleep. I told her I had come to say goodbye.

"Ah," she said. "The inevitable."

She ordered me to write her letters and stay in touch.

"Write. Don't just say you'll write."

I packed my Shaw prefaces and one or two books bought from a bookstall along the river. I packed a copy of Tropic of Cancer to sell in New York, possibly for ten times its price, from what I'd heard. Carrying my suitcase down the hotel's corkscrew stairs I passed Martine mounting the steps with a happy wide-eyed African-American climbing behind her, as pale an African as I'd ever seen with her.

I couldn't think what to say except goodbye.

"Au'voir," she said, cheerful as ever.

Off to the Gare du Nord, the boat train to Le Havre and the ship that would make the five-day crossing to New York.

Goodbye, Paris, goodbye . . .

Evening on the Île de France and to shut out the gray-black water separating me from Europe, there's thank god a library of books discarded by earlier travelers and bound now in leather I read an anthology of writings by Thomas Wolfe. The deckle-edge pages fall open to a passage about America as a "place of autumnal moons hung low and orange at the frosty edges of the pines . . . the place of the stir and feathery stumble of the hens upon their roost, the frosty, broken barking of the dogs, the great barn shapes and solid shadows in the running sweep of the moon-whited countryside, the wailing whistle of the fast express . . ." His lyricism chiming with another book's "lost Swede towns and the thrilling returning trains of youth," the phrases taking me back to my earliest years as I lay in bed in a Jersey City that now no longer exists and, hearing in the predawn quiet the clipclop of the milkman's horse and the distant mourn of a ferry crossing New York Bay. As a five-year-old I used to wonder what some of the quiet noises meant and listened in the dark to the muffled clankings of freight cars loading cargoes on to ships bound for far-off ports and try to interpret from the strangeness of the sounds what mysterious world I was living in.

And now thinking of my parents who in their passage to America years earlier walked the decks of another liner. "Oui, mod-mwazel, Non, mod-mwazel" – my mother impersonating fawning stewards pampering them on a sunny deck with English tea biscuits and Italian ices and plumping up the cushions of their deck chairs on the leisurely nine-day cruise to Americá and whatever strange new life was awaiting them in their happily traveling – and now me, not happily traveling, to whatever life awaited me.

Off-season – few passengers. Outside on an upper deck, a bistro, empty except for a heavily-made-up woman at the bar who gives me a warm smile, obviously in holiday mode. We exchange bios. Her husband, not travelling, is a minor functionary in Whitehall, and as we talk over drinks she suggestively proposes we make a fun crossing of it. I think how happy such a prospect would have made me before Cleo. But the woman's wide eye shadow of cobalt blue and the pink-candy lip gloss smeared beyond the contours of her lips make me wonder how a husband could kiss that. She asks whether I had ever thought of being a lounge lizard – and explains what lounge lizard means, saying there are women in the Upper East Side of Manhattan who pay for the company of amusing gigolos. Making my excuses for being such poor company I go below, and in the dining room that evening see her come in with a middle-aged Frenchman with a well-cared-for moustache, and after that they're seen together, lunch and dinner, till New York.

Last Day Out

Dead ahead! The hundred-story Empire State Building sticks out of an expanse of ocean like a magic skyscraper soaring surreally upward from the sea. Then, slowly, the upper stories tops of Manhattan coagulate in the water and gradually become a smudge of coastline – as now the ship slows to a lazy drift past Coney Island to enter New York Bay.

Two Frenchmen leaning on the railing beside me look down at the water sliding past and observe the clean line separating the iron-gray-black of the Atlantic and the pale brown silt of the Hudson. As we enter the brown murk of bay one says: "And they swim in that!"

Slowly-appearing New Jersey is a distant haze and the two Frenchmen prepare themselves for the Statue of Liberty, the great gift of France. I make out Liberty's arm upraised toward Europe: "Go back!"

The Frenchmen are savvy about the country's puritanism, the more experienced one teaching his companion a new American expression about working women who don't live alone.

"They live with a female friend – rrroom-mate."

"Lesbians?"

"Oh no, no, no. Just till they find husbands. It's just to share the rent till they find husbands."

New York. Not the best of times to be going back to America. War talk, all nuclear, by politicians who can't pronounce the word correctly, the country is in a state of alarm by a politics of fear. I'm back, home but not home – back to a strangeness. The odd thing is to be back at a home that feels like a strangeness. What have I done? What had I wished for by going to Paris?

After Paris everything about New York is ugly. The Metropolitan Opera House on 39th Street is a brick soot-darkened factory building. A Sunday Times article asks, "Picasso: Madman or Genius?" Newspaper columnists are completing a hatchet job on Ingrid Bergman, who has gone to live with an Italian film director. The FBI is leaking claims that Frank Sinatra is a known communist, and with all this happening, Charlie Chaplin feels it safer to stay in Europe to avoid prison.

The subway – oh that depressing sight: the sallow look on the ashen faces of young men keeping their eyes stiffly ahead to avoid being caught looking at the young women sitting opposite who too stare stiffly ahead. It is death-in-life. I'm slipping into a dark hole. There are no cafés in New York, even in the Village there are no cafes, only barrooms and sawdust saloons with small slits for front windows that are shut tight by Venetian blinds to protect the clientele from being seen by passers-by as though in having a beer they're acting immorally. In a dump of a MacDougal Street bar I feel despair for two New York University students wearing baseball caps and getting excited at glimpsing the elastic edge of a girlfriend's panties peeping over the top of the back of her skirt as she bends over. "This could be the night!" they grin at the erotic sight and one asks his friend if he was sure she would "go all the way."

I have reversed the years of my life. I had something good and have lost it. Paris was now going on without me. Cleo was going on without me. Cleo – another good thing I had lost. The best thing I had ever had – I have lost her. Only memories now. How different it had been – like the time we treated ourselves to a moules dinner and she, not yet aware I was back in the room from buying wine downstairs, had her foot on the low sill of the porte-fenètre trimming short defiant curls of her dark young woman's bush that she called "the people down south". She then straddling the bidet for a quick musical whizz so raucous against the porcelain we laughed as she rose up and hopped on one foot while fussing with a satin elastic strap on her thigh to re-anchor a nylon and finish dressing to –

I had to stop thinking such thoughts, would let myself

think of them later. Not now. Later I might write and tell her to come over and we would go on from where we had left off. That was something I could let myself think about. And that was what I should do.

While still in Jersey City I had sent out film for development, a roll of souvenir shots of Cleo before she left for Italy. Clowning on the bidet she had heaped gobs of soapy lather over her crotch, thighs spread and an impish index finger pointing comically downward toward the foam. It would be exciting and wonderful to see the images, made, as Cleo had said laughing at the time, "as something to remember me by." But when I went back for the pictures, the dealer informed me the roll of film had been confiscated by Kodak. "Kodak does not print pornography," he added as a gratuitous comment. I had to move across the river. I had to get away from moral filth.

While exploring Greenwich Village and my new neighborhood I bumped into a GI painter I had met at the Pommier. He was passing through New York on his way home to Louisville or Cincinnati and knew Jay. Yes, Jay was doing well, the Dôme was changing, no, he didn't know Yette, she was a prostitute friend? Well, well. Wished he had known her. In saying goodbye he asked, "Still painting?" the question the casual one between two people who had briefly met once and barely knew each other. He told me about a place nearby that painters went to, on University Place, the Oak Bar, if I was interested.

"Not much of a place," he said. "But it's people who make a place, isn't it?"

It was actually a gloomy barn, a barroom that could have passed for the waiting room of a small Balkan railway station where a local train came through once a week.

I made friends with the artists hanging out at this bar and their women lovers, wonderfully complaisant women drawn to the casual morals of artists. Being with them makes things seem less gloomy. Where at first I thought only a frontal lobotomy could eliminate the pain of remembering Paris, the new friendships began lessening the ache. The Village wasn't the Left Bank but it would have to do. And Cleo? With time I would slowly grow accustomed to her absence. Or I supposed I would.

I cried for the first three days I was back.

That was the end. Or so I thought until this morning, when crammed into the mailbox in my grimy vestibule, there was a mammoth-sized arty-touristy card scrunched in half as though it had been jammed with difficulty through the mail slot. It was from Cleo.

I had sent her a birthday card with my new address on it if she ever wanted to be in touch and the reply had come back from Bologna. She asked how I was finding New York and was I happy. After some silliness about Bologna, Baloney, Baudelaire and Beyond, she missed good old Manhattan and was thinking of returning for a visit to see her family in Connecticut. Did I think we could meet? Would I like to join up while she was here?

Memories of her kooky stares in mirrors surged back and I saw her lips pursing, head turning this way and that, in – what? self-admiration? Self-put-down? Was it the insecurity of the orphan wondering if she could be loved? I dismissed the image and thought to hell with all such conjectures. That was not how I wanted to see her. And besides, what did any of that matter? I preferred remembering her clattering up the stairs at the Colarossi studio with a whole pile of painting gear, her grin appearing in the doorway and she yelling, "I'm here!"

O Cleo! I have made a big mistake and will rectify it.

I scribbled a reply – yes! It would be wonderful seeing her again – and yes! we would do all sorts of things together – start a life together. Which boat will she be coming back on? I'll meet her at the dock. But how would we live? I don't know but we would surely find a way. What mattered was that we would join up.

Plastering the envelope with more stamps than needed, I dispatched the letter from the post office to insure speedy delivery. It would all work out.

She'll be here soon now and we'll be together again – as before only better. And thinking that made me happy. We would be together again, this time not to part.

/ / / / / /\\\\\

About the Author

Hiag Akmakjian is the author of several fiction and non-fiction works, including the novels *Name Dropping: The Cedar Bar In The 1950s* and *30,000 Mornings*.

Readers who would like to learn more about the narrator of Cleo will find *Name Dropping* of interest as it forms a sort of sequel to Cleo as his further life back in America is explored.

www.ingramcontent.com/pod-product-compliance
Lightning Source LLC
Chambersburg PA
CBHW070455130626
46555CB00003B/1018